TANNER'S GUNS

It's 1913. Mexico is being torn apart by revolution and the rebels need guns to oust the corrupt General Huerta in Mexico City. Elliott Blaze has an entire arsenal for sale. All he needs is trustworthy, Spanish-speaking Jake Tanner to get a tough job done . . . However, Jake and his partner in crime are soon playing cat-and-mouse with the armies of two countries. They've been double-crossed, and now face a terrifying showdown, pitted against the Mexican Army's latest secret weapon!

MATT LOGAN

TANNER'S GUNS

Complete and Unabridged

LINFORD
Leicester

First published in Great Britain

First Linford Edition
published 2010

British Library CIP Data

Whitehead, David, *1958 –*
Tanner's guns. - - (Linford mystery library)
1. Illegal arms transfers- -Mexico- -Fiction.
2. Mexico- -History- -Revolution,
1910 – 1920- -Fiction. 3. Western stories.
4. Large type books.
I. Title II. Series
823.9'14–dc22

ISBN 978–1–44480–107–1

Published by
F. A. Thorpe (Publishing)
Anstey, Leicestershire

Set by Words & Graphics Ltd.
Anstey, Leicestershire
Printed and bound in Great Britain by
T. J. International Ltd., Padstow, Cornwall

This book is printed on acid-free paper

This book is for
Thomas Knip,
With sincere thanks

1

Jake Tanner opened one gummy brown eye and looked around.

'Uhhh . . .'

In the chilly grey light of dawn the bedroom appeared drab and faded, and for a moment he couldn't remember where he was. Then it came to him. *Home*. Or at least what, over the last twelve months or so, had *become* home.

Maggie Shaw's place.

Slowly he rolled onto his back and pulled the warm cotton sheet away from his face. It seemed that his brain was taking longer and longer to wake up these days. Getting old, he guessed.

He spent another half-minute listening to Maggie's heavy, relaxed breathing. She was still buried beneath a mound of sheets beside him. Then he sat up, threw off the covers and set his bare feet down on the icy linoleum floor.

Maggie stirred slightly. When she

spoke, her voice was muffled and sluggish. ' . . . ah . . . wha' . . . ?'

Halfway through pulling his pants up, Jake growled, 'Go back to sleep. It's still early.'

He fumbled the buttons of his sky-blue shirt closed, hauled up his suspenders and then sat on the edge of the bed and eased on his scuffed stovepipe boots. After that he reached for the tobacco sack and papers scattered across the bedside cabinet and rolled himself a cigarette.

' . . . uh,' said Maggie, shifting a little, ' . . . what time is it?'

As he lit up he threw a glance at the old grandfather clock in the corner. 'Quarter of six,' he replied.

His first intake of tobacco smoke shuffled some of the phlegm around inside his chest, and the resulting coughing fit was protracted and painful. Once it had finished, however, he felt much more awake. 'I'm goin' to wash-up,' he said over his shoulder. 'Set some coffee brewin'.'

Maggie's only reply was a moan, a sigh and a short, sharp snore.

Jake quit the room quietly, favouring his left leg a little. In Maggie's small but neat kitchen, he set a fire in the stove, started the coffee cooking and pumped some cold water into the copper-lined sink. His movements were slow and sure, his breathing loud and raspy.

He took a long time washing. He scrubbed at his face until his saddle-leather skin glowed. Then he took his razor from a small pouch hanging on a hook inside the pie safe, lathered up and set about shaving. Behind him, the coffee began to bubble gently.

Jake stared hard at his reflection in the fancy little mirror Maggie always kept on the sill, trying not to cut himself as he ran the honed steel across his skin. He had an important meeting later this morning and he didn't want to turn up to it wearing a face full of cigarette papers.

The man staring back at him had a dark, lived-in face, thin in the cheeks, long in the jaw and wide in the mouth. His thinning hair was the colour of rock-dust, worn with a centre parting, and his teeth were long and yellow. He was also tall: three inches above six feet: loose-jointed too, though stiffening up a little now, as age took its toll.

He rinsed off, rubbed a towel across his face and subjected himself to one final inspection. *There*, he decided. *That should do it.*

Jake had never been one to take much pride in his appearance. In his line of work — wrangling — there'd never been much need. Nope: he'd come into the horse business as a ragamuffin kid back in '82, fifteen years old and still wet behind the ears, and he'd stuck at it instead of moving on, and finally gone out thirty years later, still a sorry-looking mess.

'Course, he thought as he went over to the table and set out two chipped china cups, he'd known all along how things would turn out. You didn't spend all those years breaking horses that didn't want to be broke without shaking something loose inside.

But every job had its risks. Jake remembered one of his old cowboy friends, Pete Hoskins, who'd almost lost a leg when a sour-tempered longhorn gored him deep from knee to ankle. And then there was Sam Fielding, who caught a bowel infection on a drive from Fort Worth to Abilene and died puking up his guts just because no-one around him knew the best way to treat his ailment.

Yes sir: every job had its risks. But you never gave them a second thought until it was too late . . .

One day about eighteen months earlier, Jake had climbed abroad a feisty little hammerhead dun to do what he'd been doing for most of his adult life, and the four-legged sonofabuck had shaken him up like a San Francisco cocktail, prancing around, swapping ends, trying to toss him over her head and crush his legs against the corral boards.

He'd stayed in the saddle for a while — later Angelo Collins told him it was seven and one-half minutes exactly — but at last he'd gone right over the nag's head and straight through two posts and four thick cross-bars.

When he woke up, Jake was on a pallet in the bunkhouse, strapped tight from head to foot. Someone had fetched Doc

Barlow from town, and he'd done the best job he could. But the damage had already been done. That feisty little horse had broken just about every bone in Jake's body, and Lord alone knew what it had done to his innards.

After that there'd been no two ways about it. Jake was finished. After three decades in the wrangling game, it was finally time to throw the key in the bucket and move on. And six months later, by which time he was just about getting around under his own steam again, he'd done just that.

But he was unemployable now. He knew no other trade but that of horse-work. His injuries, both inside and out, had slowed him down. And he wasn't too far off of fifty now: half a century. Broke up, washed up and stove in.

He'd come as far as El Paso before the money he'd received from his boss at the Slash T had run out, and then he'd kind of let himself go. Maggie Shaw had come into his life about then, though Lord knew what she saw in him or why she'd chosen to step in and halt his downward slide.

She was a widow-woman who occasionally did some cooking for one of the eateries this side of the Rio Grande, and she had a nice little adobe dwelling on the eastern fringe of town.

He still didn't know why she'd chosen to take him in, not even a year later, but he was touched by her generosity and kindness, and determined to find some way of paying her back.

He'd been twelve months trying to find a way of doing that. But maybe now, at last, he'd found one.

He poured coffee into the cups and spooned some sweetening in for Maggie. Then he carried the cups back into the bedroom and set them down on the cabinet beside her. She groaned a little beneath the rumpled sheets when he drew back the red, flowery drape and allowed the pale, slowly strengthening sunlight to flood the room. As he turned back to her with his shadow stretched across the bed, she stirred some more and finally squinted up at him through blurry blue eyes.

'Coffee,' he said, nodding toward the cups.

'Thanks.'

He watched her struggle up into a sitting position, admiring her fiercely. She was a handsome woman, meaty, the way he liked 'em. She was forty years old, and she wore her dyed blonde hair in curls and ringlets. She'd always had trouble waking up in the mornings, although that had never been a problem for Jake, and he liked seeing her while she was still a little dozy; she looked younger that way, more vulnerable, and it brought out something fatherly in him.

The first sip of coffee helped wake her up some more. By the time her eyes had cleared a bit, he was over at her cluttered dressing table, knotting a black string tie around his neck.

For a while she watched him through the shifting curtain of steam rising from the cup cradled in her hands. Then, as he pulled his buckskin jacket from the cheap wardrobe and slipped into it slowly, so's not to aggravate his arms and back, which still troubled him from time to time, she said, 'You're looking spiffy this morning.'

He threw a sober look over his

shoulder. 'Why, thank you, ma'am.'

'Going someplace special?'

He came back across the room and picked up his own cup. He'd been putting off this moment for about three days now, but he'd known he couldn't put if off forever. So he took a pull at his coffee and then said, 'Elliott Blaze ast me to look in. Says he might have a job for me.'

Her reaction was predictable. Her eyes rounded-up and she said, 'That skunk!'

'Says he might have a job for me,' Jake repeated. He turned away from her then, back to the window, beyond which El Paso was slowly coming to life.

'What kind of job?' she asked suspiciously.

He shrugged. 'I don't know, yet. That's what I'm goin' over to find out.'

'Well, whatever it is, you can be sure it's something crooked!'

'Now, you don't know that — '

He heard the sharp rustle of sheets being shoved aside as she swung out of bed. 'Well, what else is it likely to be?' she demanded. 'You know his reputation, Jake. That man's trouble!'

'Mags,' he said tiredly, turning to face her again, 'he's a man who's offerin' me a job. First damn' job I been offered in a coon's age.'

But that didn't cut any ice with her. 'Surely things can't be so desperate that you've got to take Blaze's dirty money?'

He shrugged again. 'You care to bet?'

He reached out with his free hand and gently urged her to sit down on the edge of the mattress, and he thought now that she looked every one of her forty years. Worry for him, that maybe he was mixing with the wrong sort, was ageing her even as he watched.

When she was seated again, he said, 'How long do you suppose a man who's been used to workin' all his life can live off the charity — '

'Charity be damned, Jake!'

' — off the charity of a good woman?' he finished firmly. 'Gets to the point when he don't feel like a man no more. When *I* don't feel like a man.'

'But we get by, don't we?'

'Oh sure — on what money *you* manage to pick up for us.'

10

'And you figure that throwing in with a polecat like Elliott Blaze will make things any better?'

'That'll depend on the nature of the job he's offerin',' he replied, setting his empty cup down. 'Not to mention the money.'

She looked up at him, her blue eyes searching his long, hollow face. 'Jake . . . '

'You're not gonna talk me out of it, Mags.'

'Don't you think I know that? But you're such a damned *innocent*, Jake! I just don't want to see you get used.'

He bristled, but only because he knew that what she said was true: he *was* an innocent, dammit, always ready to believe the best of a body. He'd spent most of his life that way, and he didn't guess he was going to change now.

'I won't get used, don't fret.'

Watching him cross to the door, she chewed worriedly on her bottom lip. As he set his hand down on the knob, she called his name. He looked back at her and said, 'Yeah?'

'Promise me something?'

'If it'll chase that frown off your face.'

She didn't smile, but she did pause before saying, 'Promise me you won't get involved in anything dishonest?'

He just looked at her. 'Hell, Mags. You worry too much.'

'I worry about *you*. About *us*.'

He smiled. 'Well don't. I know what I'm doin'.'

He turned again and left the room, and the pair of them knew all too well that he hadn't made the promise she'd asked for, not at all.

★ ★ ★

Jake stepped out into the new day and scanned the sky with a range-man's eye for the weather. The blue sky was broken by a few tufty white clouds, but that was all. It looked as if it was going to stay warm and dry.

El Paso was fairly bustling as he crossed the wide, dusty road and headed-up street towards the café where Maggie often worked the afternoon and evening shifts. A column of travel-stained soldiers rode by on their way to Fort

Bliss, and he paused a while on the far boardwalk to run a critical eye over their horses. A Ford truck puttered past just then, with its canvas awning shuddering, and one of the animals sidestepped a little, still nervous around these new-fangled velocipedes.

Over on the far side of the Rio Grande, where Ciudad Juarez — what Jake used to know better as El Paso del Norte — rose in a jumble of bone-white adobes, four fat Mexican women in cheap cotton dresses and *huareches* flip-flopped down to the river's edge to fetch water or rinse their washing.

He watched them for a time, then continued on up towards the café, figuring to get some breakfast before ambling over to Elliott Blaze's place.

Thinking of Blaze made him remember Maggie's warning. *A skunk*, she'd called him. *A polecat*.

Well, Jake wouldn't argue with that. Blaze was well-known as a character of dubious virtue. They said he'd learned every dirty trick there was to learn from a master, old Soapy Smith himself, the conman who'd worked his devious scams in practically every town from Leadville to Skagway, and Jake could believe it. But even Blaze must have some legitimate business interests, if only as a front behind which to disguise his more crooked undertakings. It could be that he wanted Jake to help out there.

Well, there was only one way to find out, and heck, he could always say no if he didn't care for it.

Jake reached the café and stepped inside. He saw a scattering of tables and chairs, a counter at the far end of the long, low room at which a couple of merchants were drinking coffee.

E.B. Taylor, who owned and ran the place, was just carrying two laden platters across to a pair of dusty, sun-burned stock-men as Jake closed the door behind him.

''Mornin', Jake.'

Jake nodded, hanging his black Stetson from a peg in the wall. 'E.B.'

'How's things? I ain't seen you for a couple days.'

'Oh, so-so.'

14

E.B.'s face was round and red. Sometimes he looked as if he'd spent so much time over his spitting griddle that he'd partially cooked himself. Now he wiped his hands on his greasy apron, tugged out a kerchief and mopped his brow. 'The usual?' he asked.

Jake nodded, knowing that the usual — eggs, bacon, beans and grits — would be on the house, because he lived with Maggie, and Maggie worked for E.B.

'Thanks.'

E.B. hustled back around the counter and disappeared through an arched doorway that led into the kitchen. Pots-and-pan sounds came from in there, and odd sizzlings that made his mouth water.

Jake sat at a table near the window so that he could look out into the busy main drag while he ate. A teacart trundled past, an assortment of riders, another automobile, coughing and chugging like a Baldwin on an up-grade.

It troubled him that he should have worried Maggie, troubled him also that he had deliberately avoided giving her the promise she'd asked for. She was a good woman, the best, and she deserved better. But damn, he was set on paying her back for all that she'd given him, and he'd as good as decided to take Elliott's job, whatever it was, in order to do just that.

Still, he'd never done anything illegal before. But now . . . well, face facts: he was getting old, little more than a cripple. He couldn't afford scruples any more.

Ten minutes later E.B. fetched his breakfast. It smelled good and he knew from experience that it would taste even better. But today he was so preoccupied that he hardly tasted the food at all, just chewed and swallowed more out of habit than anything else.

He didn't want to risk hurting Maggie. He *wouldn't* — intentionally. But what if he *did* get involved in something shady, and somewhere along the line it all went wrong? He'd hurt her then, for sure.

Ah, damn!

He set his cutlery down with a clatter and shoved his chair back with a loud wooden scrape. E.B. stopped chatting with the two merchants long enough to watch him grab his hat, jam it down on his head and limp out with barely a backward glance.

It was still only a little past seven o'clock, and Jake didn't suppose for one moment that Elliott Blaze was an early riser. Oh, he might live like a prince, sure, but he had no visible source of income, no job to rush off to. But what the hell: the sooner he settled this business one way or the other, the sooner he'd be able to go on back to Maggie and set her mind at rest.

Elliott's place, a two-storey structure of Spanish design, was three blocks west and two blocks south. To all four sides, wide stretches of neatly-trimmed grass distanced it from the other fine houses in the street. A neat, high picket fence further reinforced its isolation from the rest of the neighborhood.

Jake reached it after twenty minutes of slow walking, let himself through the gate and followed the wide stone path up the front door. Elliott's fancy black Pope Hartford touring car was parked to one side of the quiet *hacienda*. It had been the toast of the town when Elliott had bought it six months earlier, but already it was beginning to show signs of wear, with stone chips around the fenders and a fine layer of yellow dust covering its hood and interior.

Jake considered the vehicle for a moment, then shook his head. Progress! Autos were all right for the big cities, he decided, where they had blacktop roads everywhere. But out here the country was still largely untamed. Oh, sure, it might be 1913, but the west was still no place for cars. Horses remained the best form of transport out here, and he took a peculiar sense of comfort from the knowledge.

He yanked the bell-pull and quickly checked to make sure his tie was straight. A moment or so later the door opened and a tall, skinny Mexican in black pants, white jacket, white shirt and black tie appeared. The man was about thirty or so. A thin moustache ran the length of his upper lip.

He eyed Jake curiously as Jake took off his Stetson. '*Si?*' the Mexican said quietly.

'I'm here to see Elli — uh, Mr Blaze. Iffen he's up yet.'

'You have an appointment?'

Jake wasn't sure what an appointment was, but he had a vague notion. 'He ast me to stop by, 'bout three days ago.'

The manservant inclined his head. 'And you are . . . ?'

'Tanner,' Jake replied, extending his right hand. 'Just call me Jake.'

The Mexican pointedly ignored both the hand and the invitation. 'If you will come this way, I will see if *Señor* Blaze is taking visitors yet.' He eyed Jake disparagingly. 'It's still quite early, you know.'

Jake stepped through the door and the Mexican led him down a hallway and through an alcove into a big family room, although Elliott Blaze lived alone, and had no family worth mention.

The place was immaculate, and for a moment, Jake — who'd never even suspected that such luxury could exist — thought he'd died and gone to heaven. The fireplace was big enough to walk into. A sofa and two over-stuffed armchairs had been positioned around it.

There was a baby grand piano in the far corner and a bookcase that rose from floor to ceiling. The walls were hung with paintings — all originals, Jake noticed, no pictures clipped from Sears Roebuck catalogues like Maggie had back home: and he was absolutely entranced by the incandescent lamps spaced over the fireplace, never having come across real, genuine electric lighting before.

The Mexican told him to take a seat and he chose one of the over-stuffed armchairs before the cold, spotless hearth. As he sank down into the soft, satiny cushions, he didn't believe he would ever find it a strain to be rich, not if this was how a man could live.

But what did that man have to do in order to live so high? Sell his soul to the Devil? Jake pondered that thought as he sat there, surrounded by so much opulence, and decided that even that might be worth considering if it meant that he could give back a little of what Maggie Shaw had given him.

'Good morning, Jake! By God, you're an early bird, aren't you?'

Jake turned his head just as Elliott Blaze came in through the alcove with a cup in one hand and a saucer in the other. Blaze was wearing expensive white pants and a collarless white shirt open at the throat. Jake pushed up out of the chair to meet him, twisting his Stetson nervously in his calloused hands.

''Mornin', Elliott. Sorry if I busted in on you too early — '

'Nonsense!' said Blaze, smiling. 'I like a man who's keen.' He raised his cup. 'Coffee?'

'Ah, no thanks.'

'Just want to get straight down to cases, eh?'

'Well, somethin' like that. It's just that, I been thinkin' . . . might as well come right to the point, I guess. This here job you mentioned . . . '

Elliott Blaze waved him back to the chair he'd just vacated. 'For heaven's sake, Jake, relax! This isn't an interview. 'Far as I'm concerned, you've already *got* the job.'

Jake was too agitated to sit down again, although Blaze crossed the expensive

Oriental rug in a pair of long strides and sank down on the sofa.

'It's just . . . well, maybe we ought to get one thing straight before you tell me anything about what you got planned.'

Blaze finished his coffee and set his cup and saucer aside. In his way, he was as impressive as the house in which he lived. He was just under six feet tall and solidly put-together. His tanned face appeared almost boyish in the clean, bright sunlight that filled the room, despite the fact that he was in his late thirties. His black hair was slicked flat to his head and fashionably oiled, and his thin eyebrows were perfectly arched above his clear hazel eyes. His nose was long and straight, his lips full and animated, his jaw firm and square.

He, like his manservant, wore a pencil-thin moustache along his upper lip. He ran his left index finger along the moustache now as he eyed Jake speculatively. 'I guess you want to know how much it pays,' he said.

Jake shook his head. 'No sir,' he replied quietly. 'But I'd say it's best you know right off that, was you thinkin' to hire me for anythin' crooked, well, maybe you'd be better off findin' someone else to handle it.'

Blaze didn't bat an eyelid, but after a moment or so he smiled a little. He knew the kind of reputation he had around El Paso, knew how it could often intimidate law-abiding folks, too.

'Well, that's fair enough, I guess,' he allowed with a low chuckle. 'But I'm sorry you feel that way, Jake, because I had three reasons for wanting to deal you in on this. You're honest, you know mules, and you speak Spanish.'

Jake turned his Stetson some more. 'It *is* somethin' crooked then,' he said. 'Meanin' no offense.'

Blaze shrugged elegantly. 'Well, that depends on what you mean by *crooked*,' he replied. 'Look, I'll be straight with you, Jake, because I know you can keep your mouth shut. All right — it *is* crooked. But a week from now, or a month, and it'll be as legal as new money. Still, never let it be said that I led an honest man astray.'

He rose from the sofa and offered his hand.

'Don't let me waste any more of your time, Jake. And don't fret about any of this. No hard feelings, right? You know, if truth be told, I admire you for it. Can't be too many men willing to pass up the chance to earn five hundred dollars for three days' work, just on account of their principles.'

Jake felt his jaw drop. 'Did you ... ' Something caught in his throat and he had to swallow hard. 'Did you s-say five hundred dollars?'

Elliott nodded.

'For three days' work?'

'That's right.'

Jake turned his hat faster between his long fingers. Suddenly he started having second thoughts about this.

'Uh ... what, ah ... I mean ... just out of, uh, curiosity, what would a man have to do to pick up that kind of money?'

Elliott met his gaze. He looked absolutely sure of himself, standing there in cool white, tanned, athletic, urbane. He knew that the prospect of earning so much cash had hooked Jake good. But still he paused a while before replying.

'Maybe it's best you *don't* know.'

Jake rubbed his jaw with one hand. 'Well . . . what I mean is, would it be *bad* crooked, or just *crooked* crooked. You know: it wouldn't be nothin' like a stick-up, or some kind'a strongarm work . . . would it?'

Elliott's smile broadened. 'No, nothing like that.'

Jake drew in a deep breath, just to steady himself against a sudden feeling of lightheadedness. 'All right,' he said, taking the plunge. 'So long as it's nothin' too tough, count me in, Elliott. For five hundred bucks — I'm your man.'

2

This time, when Elliott told him to sit, Jake sat. Then Elliott called for his manservant and ordered fresh coffee, and while they waited, Jake said, 'So . . . what's it all about then, this job?'

Elliott said candidly, 'Gun-running.'

Jake drew in a sharp breath. 'Ah . . . don't get me wrong, Elliott, but . . . that sounds like it could be risky.'

'Why did you think the pay was so good?'

That was a good point. 'Okay,' Jake said, still game despite his inner misgivings. 'Let's hear it.'

'I need to deliver a shipment of weapons to a customer across the border, *pronto*.'

'What's the hurry?'

'Well, apart from anything else, it's a cash-on-delivery deal, so the sooner my customer gets his guns, the sooner I get paid. But there's another reason too.'

Elliott sat back on the sofa and crossed his legs. 'How much do you know about this revolution they're having down south?'

Jake shrugged. He knew very little. The Mexicans were always up in arms about something. After a while it got so a man just didn't pay much attention any more. 'Not a lot,' he confessed.

'Well, I don't suppose there's any reason why you should,' Elliott replied. 'On the surface, at least, what happens over the line doesn't affect us one way or the other.'

'But?'

As briefly as he could, Elliott ran through the events which had led to his present situation.

The Revolution had started three years earlier, when, having seen enough of the brutality and repression of President Diaz' tyrannical government, a wealthy Creole idealist named Francisco Madero called his brothers to arms with a book entitled *The Presidential Succession*. The resulting struggle had been long, hard and bloody, but in 1911 Diaz was finally ousted and, after the short reign of Francisco Leon de la Barra, Madero had been elected president.

Earlier this year, however, Madero and his vice-president, Pino Suarez, had been betrayed by the very man Madero had made his Minister of War, General Victoriano Huerta. Huerta had executed the two politicians and promptly set himself up as a leader every bit as tyrannical as Porfirio Diaz.

'But I'd hate to be in Huerta's boots right now,' Elliott went on grimly. 'Because this time, the people really *have* had enough of dictators.'

Huerta's most powerful opponents had formed an admittedly-uneasy alliance in order to bring him down. To the south lay the guerrilla army of Emiliano Zapata. To the north were massed the forces of the bandit leader Pancho Villa. The governor of Coahuila Province, Venustiano Carranza, was also part of the coalition: his army was under the command of a *ranchero* named Alvaro Obregon.

'Villa and Zapata are planning to

march on Mexico City,' Elliott con-
cluded. 'But they need weapons if they're
to succeed, good, reliable weapons, not
the poorly-maintained antiques they're
making do with at the moment.'

'And you're the feller who can supply
'em?'

The Mexican manservant, Miguel,
entered the room with a tray in his hands.
Crockery made little tinkling sounds as
he set the tray down and wordlessly began
to pour coffee.

Elliott, answering Jake's question, said,
'Yes: I'm the fellow who can supply
them.' He sat forward and took the cup
Miguel offered him. 'My customer is
Pancho Villa himself, a bit of a rough
diamond, but trustworthy enough. I've
done business with him before. He has
agents who'll take delivery of the weapons
in Los Caballos Mestenos four days from
now.'

'And where in hell is Los Caballos
Mestenos?'

'About seventy miles south of El Paso,'
Elliott replied. 'It should be a straightforward enough run. All you've got to do is

deliver the goods, collect the money and bring it back here.'

'You're sure you can trust these here Mexicans not to double-cross you?'

'I'm sure,' Elliott said sincerely. 'As I say, I've had dealings with them before. They're hardly likely to kill the golden goose.' He took a sip from his cup. 'Well, Jake? Are you still in?'

Jake took a cup from the manservant. 'You still haven't told me why you're in such a blamed hurry to get the guns delivered yet,' he reminded.

Elliott sat back again. 'Oh, that's simple. At the moment, the *revolucionarios* can only get their guns and ammunition through sources such as myself. That means I can buy cheap here and sell dear over the line. But I've recently heard a pretty strong rumour that President Wilson's considering lifting the U.S. arms embargo. If he does that — '

' — the Mexicans won't have no more need for you,' Jake finished. 'They'll be able to buy cheap for themselves.' He spent a moment running it all through his mind. 'So that's why you said this deal might be crooked one day an' legal the next.'

'Exactly.'

Jake busied himself with some more careful thought. As risky as he'd always considered gun-running to sound, this particular deal sure seemed safe enough. Furthermore, if President Wilson himself was thinking about relaxing the arms embargo, supplying weapons to the Mexicans couldn't be *too* dishonest, could it?

He gulped down some coffee. He knew he was only splitting hairs, that Maggie would probably never see it that way, but . . .

Again he thought about the money: five hundred dollars for three days' work. It was an opportunity that few men would — or could — turn down.

'Jake,' Elliott said, breaking in on his ruminations. 'I asked you a question a moment ago. You haven't answered it yet. Are you still in, or what?'

'Sure I'm in,' Jake replied, sounding more confident about his decision than he actually felt. 'Just how many weapons are you figurin' to move, anyway?'

'Fifty Springfield rifles,' Elliott replied.

Jake nodded. 'All right. We — '

'One hundred Winchester carbines,' Elliott went on. 'The box magazine models of '95.'

'All right. Let's suppose — '

'Twenty-five Mauser pistols,' Elliott continued, deadpan. 'And the same number of Colts.'

Jake eyed the younger man sidelong. 'Is that all?' he asked.

Elliott shook his head. 'No. There's ammunition enough for the lot.'

'Oh.'

'And . . . '

'And?'

'And a dozen Lewis machine guns, complete with tripods.'

Jake snorted. 'Caesar's ghost, Elliott: you sure don't do things by halves! Just how much is this little batch gonna net you?'

Elliott said calmly, 'Ten thousand dollars.'

'Ten — ! An' you're figurin' to pay me — '

'Take it or leave it, Jake. I don't have time to argue about it.'

Jake fell silent. He knew better than to hold out for more money. There were some men you just didn't dicker with, and Elliott Blaze was one of them. Instead, he made a few quick mental calculations.

'These guns,' he said. 'They're all boxed up?'

'Uh-huh. They've all been packed in cosmoline-filled crates, same with the ammo.'

'I'd say you'll need about fifteen mules, then.'

'All right. See to it, and take Miguel with you. You pick 'em, he'll pay for 'em.'

'I'd also say I'll need some help along the way. Another man.'

That obviously didn't set well with Elliott. 'I'd as soon not involve too many people,' he remarked.

'Well, that's up to you. But it's too much responsibility for one man. If anythin' happens to me, the guns won't get through. An' somethin' *could* happen, Elliott. The cavalry run regular patrols along the border, just in case your friend Villa comes araidin', an' there's all manner of other *bandidos* infest the Big Bend country.'

Elliott mulled that over. 'Got anyone in mind?'

'Not yet. But I can probably scare someone up for the job.'

'Just so long as you can trust him with my money, Jake: *and* to keep his mouth shut.'

Jake nodded. 'Rely on it. I don't want to get caught any more'n you do.'

They talked over a few more points. There was, of course, an awful lot to go through: how much Elliott would pay the second man, the best time for Jake to make his border crossing and so on. It took quite a while, but at the end of it Jake and the Mexican manservant, Miguel, went to purchase the pack-mules.

Jake started taking his responsibilities even more seriously now. He was, after all, committed to seeing this business through. And though Elliott had assured him that the risks were minimal, Jake figured to see that they stayed that way.

So, once they were out on the street, he suggested that they buy their mules in twos and threes from a number of different horse-traders, so's not to arouse too much suspicion.

As the morning wore on, they toured the stables, made their purchases and promised to come back later to collect the animals. Along with the mules, they bought pack-trees, which would make the loading and unloading of the guns that much easier. They also purchased a strong-limbed blood bay horse for Jake and a more docile, but firmly-built, piebald for the second man — whoever he should turn out to be.

When they were finished, and Miguel was busily brushing dust off his crisp white jacket, Jake suggested they go wet their whistles at Bernie Woolcott's Gilded Cage Saloon. Miguel slowly looked him up and down, appearing scandalized by the idea, then excused himself, saying that he still had other chores to tend, notably purchasing the supplies Jake would need for his forthcoming trip.

Well and truly put in his place, Jake

watched the prissy Mexican stride off down the boardwalk, haughty as hell, and shook his head. Sometimes servants could be a damn'-sight more high-hat than the folks who employed them.

Still, there was no denying it: he could sure use a drink. The street was a riot of noise and motion, and right now Jake wanted a little peace and quiet to organise his thoughts. He began to head for the Gilded Cage at a steady limp, figuring that, if nothing else, it might be a good place to find that second man he was looking for. At the very least, he could brace himself with a couple of whiskies before going home and breaking the news to Maggie.

He pushed through the frosted-glass doors and stepped in off the street fifteen minutes later. The saloon was almost empty, but he'd half-expected that. It was only mid-morning, after all: the place wouldn't start to liven up much until noon or thereabouts.

At the moment there was one man up at the walnut bar washing down free lunch sandwiches with lukewarm beer, and a card game going on at a corner table. Jake shuffled across thirty feet of sawdust-covered floor to get to the bar. There were tables and chairs dotted everywhere, and because it was still relatively early, most of the chairs were still up-ended on the tables. A staircase rose up to a gallery at the far end of the bar, and along the north wall a Pianola was playing a merry rendition of *Buffalo Gals*.

Bernie Woolcott was shifting barrels about behind the bar. Because he was a small man, he was finding it heavy going. His long, wrinkled face was red, and the high colour made his lumpy, drinker's nose look not unlike a strawberry.

As he bellied up to the bar, Jake dug into his pants'-pocket for some change and said, 'Shot of Tangle Leg when you're ready, Bern.'

Bernie, still struggling down the far end of the bar, said, 'Help yourself. You know where it is.'

Jake let himself through the trap-door and did just that, working the cast-iron till in order to drop some coins into the drawer when he was done. He made no move to go back around to the customer's side of the bar. He was comfortable enough right where he was, and he knew that Bernie didn't mind.

He took one sip of whiskey, then pulled his string tie loose and unbuttoned his blue shirt collar. 'Hot work,' he commented as Bernie straightened up from the barrel he'd just wrestled into position under the bar.

'You can say that again.'

'You ought to get someone in to handle all the heavy liftin' for you. You're gettin' too old for it.'

'You offerin'?'

'Hell, no, I'm as old as you if I'm a day, an' stove-up to boot. I'm just sayin', is all. It's not as if you can't afford it.'

Bernie pointed to the bottle of Tangle Leg Jake had left on the bartop. His narrow chest was pumping like a bellows. 'Pour me a shot of that an' send it down, will you?'

As he did so, Jake noticed that the little saloon-keeper with the red face and sandy hair was rubbing his left knee. 'What's up? You pulled somethin'?'

Bernie shook his head, deftly catching the glass Jake slid along the bar towards him. 'Naw, damn' knee always aches when we got rain on the way.'

'Rain? Are you kidding? There's hardly a cloud out there.'

'There will be,' Bernie replied, tossing the drink down in one go. 'By midnight, I reckon. This here knee ain't never played me wrong before.' His eyes lit up as a smile suddenly twitched at his mouth. 'Say, you care to have a little wager on it, Jake?'

'Thanks, but no thanks. I got just enough money on me for one more drink, an' then I'm cleaned out.'

As Bernie surveyed his handiwork, and his laboured breathing gradually settled down, Jake asked if any of the boys had been in yet. 'The boys' were those few older waddies whose advanced years had rendered them practically unemployable. They often congregated at Bernie's place, about six of them, just to spend a few hours nursing drinks and reminiscing about the old days.

Bernie shook his head. 'Ain't seen 'em in two, three days now.'

'Oh.'

'Keep an eye on things while I go fetch another barrel?'

'Sure.'

Jake watched the other man vanish through a curtained break in the back-bar wall that led out to the storeroom. He sipped carefully at his drink. The Tangle Leg was strong stuff, brewed from tobacco, molasses and peppers, and the last thing he wanted to do now was go staggering home to Maggie three sheets to the wind.

Glancing around, he eyed the man a little way along the bar, who was still chewing on the free lunch sandwiches. From the look of the dried squares of bread, they seemed to need a heap of chewing before a man dared to swallow one.

He moved his brown eyes a little, so that he could focus on the table at which the poker game was in progress. Four men were seated there, doing their best to play an interesting game of straight draw.

Jake knew three of them, though not well: they were itinerant cowboys, all big-boned and heavily-muscled, the oldest about forty or so, the youngest just leaving his twenties behind him.

Jake didn't recognize the fourth man at all. He was in his early twenties, fresh-faced and neatly barbered, with oiled brown hair and a pleasing, if innocent, smile. Unlike the cattlemen, who wore rough workaday clothes and pistols hitched high around their waists, the youngster was garbed in a creased seersucker suit. He'd placed his natty straw hat on top of a bulging suitcase beside him.

For a time Jake just listened to the odd mutterings coming from around the table as the men ante'd up. About twenty-odd dollars sat in the centre of the table, so there was a lot to play for. Then, as his thoughts returned to Maggie and the confrontation he knew he was heading for, he turned away and poured himself a second jolt of rotgut.

He was just slipping the last of his loose change into the cash drawer when the poker game drew to a close. One of the cowhands, Russ Thompson, threw in his hand with a good-natured grin. The second, Riley Wilson, set his own cards down face-up and announced, 'Two pairs.'

It was Stinky Bill Anderson who wore the look of a winner. He laid his cards down with great deliberation and said around a mouthful of discoloured, snaggle-edged teeth, 'Flush.'

Stinky Bill reached for the pot.

Folks called him Stinky because he'd grown up in the last of the buffalo towns, where the hides of those great, shaggy beasts had been piled into walls twelve to fifteen feet high prior to being shipped off East. The smell of all that death had never quite washed off of Stinky, hence the nickname. He was a decent enough fellow when he chose to be. Other times, though — most times, in fact — he could be a bully and a braggart.

Now, just a heartbeat before his big, gnarled fists closed around the money, the young man in the seersucker suit lay his cards out on the table. Quite politely he said, 'Do tell me if I'm wrong, won't you, but . . . isn't this what they call a full house?'

It went very quiet around the table and Jake turned around, craning his neck to get a better look for himself. His thin lips moved silently as he identified the young man's hand: four of hearts, clubs and spades, nine of hearts, nine of spades. Yep, full house, all right.

Russ Thompson confirmed it with a nod, but Stinky Bill just kept staring at the cards. Finally the youngster reached forward for the money, grinning broadly. 'If you'll excuse me, Mr Anderson. A full house beats a flush, I believe.'

That was true. But Stinky Bill obviously didn't care to see it that way. He had his black heart set on all those wrinkled bills and softly-glittering coins piled in the centre of the table.

Still, there wasn't much he could do about it now. Like the kid had said, a full house beat a flush every time.

Still, Stinky Bill Anderson had never been a graceful loser; especially when the feller who'd beat him was a dude damn'-near half his age — and with a weird accent to boot.

That was probably why he suddenly said, 'No.'

The kid's smile turned upside-down. 'I beg your pardon?'

Stinky Bill's eyes shuttled up to his face. He had hard, scheming eyes, and the kind of lumpy, be-whiskered face that had been sculpted by a lifetime spent rough-housing. His thick lips twitched once, and his tongue came out to wet them.

'You're wrong,' he said in a low voice. 'Flush beats ever'thin' except a straight. Ain't that right, fellers?'

He was putting his two companions in an awkward spot, because although they hung around with him and obviously found his company to their liking, neither of them had quite such a sour, scheming temperament, and no real desire to fool the kid out of his rightful winnings. Russ Thompson squirmed a little in his chair, and Riley Wilson muttered something noncommittal.

But the kid already knew he was being

flim-flammed. In a low, steady voice he said, 'Meaning no offense, Mr Anderson, but I beg to differ.'

'Oh?' Bill arched one eyebrow. 'So you fancy yourself as an expert, do yuh? How long you been playin' this here game, boy?'

'About four months.'

'Well, I been playin' it fer more'n thirty years. An' I say that a flush beats a full house. Which means,' and here his eyes grew hooded, 'that that there pot is mine.'

Jake watched the kid closely, wondering if he should lend a hand before things took a more dangerous turn. A little way down the counter, the fellow eating all the free lunch sandwiches also paused, but only to take a pull at his beer mug.

Before Jake could act one way or the other, the youngster shook his head. 'I really am dreadfully sorry about this,' he said, sounding as if he meant it. 'But you really *are* mistaken, Mr Anderson. You see, there are approximately five thousand, one hundred and eight different ways in which a flush can be made up. The number of possible combinations that form a full house, however, are considerably less — about three thousand . . . seven hundred and . . . forty-four, I believe. So you see, you're quite wrong, old boy. Your flush can be beaten by a straight flush: fours, which you appear to have forgotten: and, of course — a full house.'

Stinky Bill failed to understand most of that. So did Jake. But he got the meaning behind the words clearly enough: the kid knew that Bill was trying to dupe him out of his money, and he wasn't having it. That left Bill with two choices. And since he wasn't going to back down and kiss the loot goodbye, he chose to employ a little intimidation.

He stood up. It was a remarkable thing to see. He was six and a half feet tall, and his high-heeled boots pushed him to perhaps six-eight. His thick arms stretched at the seams of his grubby plaid shirt, and his barrel chest strained at the row of little black buttons running down the front. Wearing his most threatening scowl, he said, 'Now, let's get this straight, boy. I say I'm right. You say I'm wrong. That means you're callin' me a cheat — right?'

Russ Thompson said, 'Aw, leave it, Bill — '

'Or a liar?'

From the other side of the bar, Jake said, 'Anderson . . . '

The youngster in the seersucker suit also got to his feet. He was about five feet ten in his flat walking boots, and of average build. He said, 'I'm calling you nothing of the sort, Mr Anderson. But if the cap fits . . . '

'Why, you lippy little — '

Seeing Bill's hand dropping to his holstered Colt, Riley Wilson said, 'For God's sake, Bill, the kid's unarmed!'

To which Bill replied, 'Well . . . he's got fists, don't he?'

He didn't really expect an answer, so he didn't bother waiting for one. He just grabbed the edge of the table and shoved it aside, spilling his two friends backwards, and the thin wooden table-legs shuddered across the sawdusted plank floor with a sound like the opening of a coffin-lid.

47

Then, without warning, Bill was upon his shorter, lighter adversary, all fists and curses. The kid ducked under Bill's first roundhouse right and went to dance aside, bringing his own fists up in the classic prize-fighter's stance. He looked mighty confident, too: but unfortunately he'd forgotten all about the bulging suitcase sitting beside him.

He tripped over it and stumbled five feet across the room, struggling to retain his balance. Stinky Bill came right after him, crushing the kid's straw hat underfoot. His second punch caught the kid right on the ear and sent him reeling still further with the side of his face glowing bright crimson.

'That's enough!' barked Jake, but he doubted that Bill even heard him. The big bruiser was going after the kid like the Devil after a crippled saint. He caught him with a left jab and sent him crashing into another table.

Up-ended chairs spilled everywhere. Then he grabbed the kid by one blue-striped lapel and hit him right in the stomach. The kid doubled up like a broken doll, and Jake figured he'd seen enough. Bill's two partners might be too scared of him to intervene, but Jake had never found much pleasure in watching other folks — particularly the kind who couldn't defend themselves — take lumps.

He got as far as the trap-door, near which the fellow chewing the free lunch sandwiches was still munching stoically. Then he drew up as the kid somehow got his breath back and managed to land one small, smooth fist right on the point of Bill's granite jaw.

The blow should have done a lot more damage than it did. On any other man it probably would have. But Bill wasn't like any other man. Bill was . . . well, *Bill*. The blow had no effect on him whatsoever. It didn't even rock him back on his heels.

The kid, by contrast, looked as if he'd been struck by lightning. Shaking his hand to get some feeling back into it, he said, very clearly, '*Ow!*'

Then Bill reached down, snatched him up, spat into his bloodied face and tossed him aside. The kid hit another table and more up-ended chairs fell like skittles.

At last Bernie Woolcott hurried back from the storeroom and demanded, 'For cryin' out loud, what's goin' on here?'

Jake would have told him had he not chosen that exact moment to shuffle hurriedly around the counter and yell, 'All right, Anderson! That's enough, I say!'

Bill heard him then, and halted his advance on the kid, who was sprawled half-on, half-off the table, looking distinctly green about the gills. At first he had trouble placing Jake. Then Jake saw recognition sharpen the other man's gaze.

'It's Tanner, ain't it?' Bill growled in a low voice.

Jake swallowed hard, then said, 'Yeah. Now leave the kid be an' haul freight, Bill. He won that money fair an' square, an' you know it.'

Bill stuck out his bottom lip belligerently. 'Aw, butt out, gimp.'

Jake immediately drew himself up. 'Why don't you *make* me?' he countered.

He stared hard at the other man. He'd often heard it said that all bullies like

Stinky Bill needed was someone to stand up to them. They were bluster, the lot of 'em. Once you called their bluff, all the hot air went out of them and they backed down.

'Well?' Jake demanded, forcing some steel into his tone. 'What's it to be, Bill? You puttin' up, or *shuttin'* up?'

Bill clenched his fists again and came at Jake with his face set like a promise of pain, and Jake thought dismally, *Aw, nuts!*

It looked like Bill was puttin' up.

3

As he came at Jake, he made a low roaring sound like an enraged bull, and Jake did exactly what he would've done had a bull been storming towards him right at that moment. He got out of the way, fast.

As Stinky Bill thundered down on him he lunged aside. Bill went blundering by, pulled up almost at once and twisted around with his right arm drawn back for another roundhouse.

Before he could launch it, Jake lashed out with a punch of his own. It caught Bill on one cauliflower ear and bounced off, and as the pain of it shot through the bigger man's head, Jake hit him again and again, left, right, left, right, determined to press his advantage, and frankly too damn' scared to do anything else.

Dimly he heard Bernie Woolcott yelling that enough was enough. Russ Thompson was echoing much the same sentiment.

Then Stinky Bill came up against the walnut bar, and with nowhere else to go, started hitting back.

He caught Jake a glancing blow that caused him more surprise than hurt. But surprise was all that Bill needed, because it put Jake off his stride for just a moment, and bought him all the few brief seconds he required to recover. He came at Jake again then, and his devastating barrage of lefts and rights rocked Jake slowly back towards the centre of the room.

Behind the bar, Bernie did some more screeching. The man at the free lunch counter swallowed the last sandwich on the plate and finished his beer as calm as you like, then turned and started edging around the wall to get to the door.

Jake's thoughts, meanwhile, were beginning to jumble up into a confused tangle. He tasted blood in his mouth, felt a warm line of it spill down across his chin. Frantically he tried to block his opponent's blows. He countered one, two, one more, but Bill's fighting blood was up now and he was damned if he'd call it a day just yet.

He caught Jake with another left jab, and this time Jake shoved the hurt of it aside just long enough to lash out in retaliation. His blow landed on Bill's nugget-shaped nose and left it stinging. Bill made a noise that sounded a little like, '*I'llgetyouforthayousonofabitch!*', and then proceeded to do exactly that.

He rushed Jake and grabbed him by the front of his shirt and the crotch of his pants, and Jake gave a strangulated cry as Bill hoisted him overhead.

'Bill!' yelled Russ Thompson.

'Fer God's sake — !' cried Riley Wilson.

Jake didn't weigh much, despite his height. So, for a man of Bill Anderson's strength, it was a small enough feat. But throwing Jake right across the bar and into the bottle-lined shelves nailed up on the backbar wall took considerably more effort.

Not that Jake was in any position to appreciate it. The minute Bill had him, he knew he was in serious trouble. Then he hit the shelves and all of a sudden Bernie was shouting in a much higher key.

Jake smashed against the shelves and bottles smashed against him. He might have bawled a curse but he wasn't sure. Then he dropped out of sight behind the bar in a shower of fragmented glass and sweet-smelling alcohol, and landed with a thump.

For a while the noise was tremendous men yelling, glass shattering, the low *glug-glug-glug* of brandy escaping from an over-turned bottle, and of course the Pianola belting out a big finish to *Buffalo Gals*.

Then the music came to an end and it fell eerily silent, and no-one could really decide which was worse. They all stood where they were, even Stinky Bill, who was thinking that maybe he'd gone a little too far this time.

It seemed to take an eternity for the brandy bottle to empty out, but when it did, and it was so quiet in the Gilded Cage Saloon that you could've heard an angel's belch, Bill said, 'T-Tanner?'

There was no reply.

'Judas, Bill, you've killed him!' husked Riley Wilson, looking white-faced.

Bill turned his head and glared at him. 'Killed 'im be damned!' he snapped. 'He's likely just unconscious is all.'

Again he returned his attention to the bar, beyond which lay the wreckage of about fifty bottles of booze, and one stove-up wrangler.

'Tanner? You . . . you all right, feller?'

Nothing.

Bill Anderson licked his blood-stained lips. Slowly he approached the bar, thinking, *Oh my Gawd, don't tell me I've actually gone an' kilt 'im . . .*

He bellied up to the bar. The stink of all that mixing alcohol was sickening. 'T-Tanner?' he asked, leaning across the counter. 'John, is it? Or Jake? Jake? Ol' buddy . . . ?'

Jake suddenly came up from behind the bar, hatless and soaked through with everything from sarsaparilla to Doc Sizewell's Liver Regulator.

Then he grabbed the front of Bill's plaid shirt in one hand and cracked him over the head with the wheel-spoke he held in the other.

Wood met skull with a dull popping sound. Bill went down with a grunt and a sigh, about as out for the count as a man could get without actually up and dying. He landed hard with a thud and started to snore.

'Hot-damn,' said the man who'd just finished off the free lunch sandwiches.

Jake tossed the wheel-spoke aside and turned to Bernie, who was just standing there shaking his head in disbelief at all the damage to his premises.

'Mighty handy pacifier you got there, Bern,' Jake remarked, nodding to the thick length of wood.

Bernie said numbly, 'Mighty . . . pacifier . . . ?'

Then some of his shock wore off and his voice grew a little stronger. 'Aw, fer . . . jus' look at this place! *Look* at it! You've ruined me, you fellers! My stock, my shelves . . . '

Jake suddenly held tightly to the edge of the bar as his legs turned spongy beneath him. For a moment his arms and back ached so much that he had to clench his teeth to stop from passing out.

Stinky Bill's two buddies hustled over and eyed him with concern. 'You all right, Tanner?' asked Thompson.

Jake nodded. 'I'll live.' He winced. '*Just*. How 'bout the kid?'

'Oh . . . ah . . . I . . . I'm fine, thank you.'

Bernie swore a couple of times, then reverted to more moderate language in order to say again, 'Just look at this place!'

The kid, satisfied that his jaw was neither broken nor unhinged, said, 'There's twenty-seven dollars and forty one cents on that far table, Mr Woolcott. I insist that you put it toward the cost of your repairs.'

Bernie was somewhat less than grateful. 'Twenty-seven dollars won't go far,' he grumbled sourly.

'We'll chip in the rest,' said Riley Wilson, digging into his pocket. 'Bill c'n pay us back later.'

'Talkin' of Bill,' Russ Thompson cut in, also checking his pockets for cash, 'I'm thinkin' you'd better make tracks, Tanner.

When Bill wakes up an' his head stops palpitatin', he's gonna come a-lookin' fer you.'

Jake nodded. That was probably true. But since he was going to be out of town for a few days anyway, the chances were good that Bill would eventually simmer down and forget all about it.

Still, he said wearily, 'Yeah, I guess I will be pushin' along. Uhh . . . '

Thompson frowned at him. 'You sure you're all right?'

'Yeah. Reckon I been achin' so long, a few more smarts won't make much difference.'

Even so, Jake's movements were slower than usual as he dragged himself around the counter, leaving the rest of them to it. He was feeling tired now, real tired, and the sweet stink coming off his damp clothes was positively noisome. All those itchy little glass cuts in his face weren't helping much, either. He pulled a kerchief from his pocket, mopped his face and brought the square of cloth away red.

'Excuse me, sir.'

Jake turned to the kid. He was in his

59

early twenties, pale-faced, handsome and personable, but right now he looked as rough around the edges as Jake felt. He came up to Jake and offered his hand.

'I'm really very grateful to you, Mr, ah . . . Tanner, was it? If you'll pardon my language, that cheeky sod would have beaten me black and blue had you not intervened. It was very chivalrous of you, and I'm eternally in your debt.'

Jake frowned. 'You're not from around these parts, are you?'

The kid's smiled widened. 'No sir. Bagshot.'

Jake looked blank.

'That's in Surrey,' said the kid.

Still Jake looked blank.

'England,' explained the kid. As they shook hands he said, 'My name's Stanford-Brown, by the way. Harry Stanford-Brown.'

'Good to know you, Harry,' Jake said, not especially bothered one way or the other. 'Now, if you don't mind . . . ' He peeled his damp shirt away from his skin. 'I gotta go take an all-over bath afore I show up back home.'

Harry Stanford-Brown's clear blue eyes took on a shine. 'I say!' he said. 'That sounds like a capital notion, Mr Tanner! Do you mind if I join you?'

Jake looked at him suspiciously. 'I gave up sharin' baths when I was eight years old, boy,' he growled.

The young Englishman said equably, 'That's all right. I've never shared a bath with anybody in my entire *life*, and have no intention of starting the practice now.'

Behind them, Bill began to mumble and stir sluggishly. Jake sighed and said, 'All right: come on then, Harry. But you're payin' for this little luxury, you got that? I just remembered — as of that last shot of popskull I had, I'm stony broke.'

'Fair enough,' Harry said with a nod. 'Lead on, old boy.'

The Englishman retrieved his straw hat, tried his best to knock it back into shape, then grabbed up his suitcase and followed Jake out of the saloon and across the busy street.

Jake knew he dared not go home smelling like a brewery. He'd also have to do something about his face, too, because

Maggie disapproved of fighting just about as much as she disapproved of drinking.

As they stepped up onto the far boardwalk he cursed his luck. It wasn't bad enough that he was heading for a wrangle with the one woman he hated like hell to argue with: he was going to make the matter considerably worse by turning up looking like something the cat'd drug in.

He felt Harry's eyes on him. The kid could doubtless sense his mood. But he just kept heading for Per Grønmark's barbershop, where they did a good, hot bath with a chunk of lye soap thrown in, all for sixty cents. He didn't feel like talking: he was too preoccupied for that.

'Are you sure you're feeling all right, Mr Tanner?' the Englishman asked after a moment.

'Sure.'

'No broken bones or anything?'

'None.'

'It's just . . . well, you're limping, old boy.'

Jake glanced down at him at last and cracked a rare smile. 'Kid,' he said, 'I was limpin' *before* that little fracas.'

Harry appeared relieved. 'Oh. I'd have offered to treat you to a doctor's examination,' he said, 'but after I've paid for these baths we're going to have, I'm afraid I'm going to be as financially bereft as you.'

Jake looked at the kid with new interest. 'Are you sayin' you're broke too?'

'Yes.'

They walked on, skirting around a pair of women talking and a store-clerk pushing a hand-cart.

'Little off your usual stampin' grounds, ain't you, Harry?' Jake remarked. 'What brings you out here — iffen it's not too personal, that is?'

'Not at all,' Harry replied with a laugh. 'What brings me here? Two things, really. An ambition — and some bad timing.'

'Care to explain that?'

'Certainly. You see, I came over from England in order to write for the moving pictures.'

'Eh?'

'You know. Moving pictures. Movies. *Films*. Yes?'

Jake thought about it. He remembered seeing a hopelessly-phony moving picture entitled *The Great Train Robbery* with some of the Slash T hands about four years earlier. Halfway through, the film had snapped and they'd all retired to the Hungry Dog Saloon in Fort Worth to pursue a far more interesting time.

'Yeah,' he said. 'Go on.'

'Well, that was the ambition,' Harry sighed. 'But when I finally reached New York City, I discovered that all the kinematograph companies had moved west.'

'How far west?'

'Right across to the other side of the country. California. A place called Holyrood or Hollywood or something.'

'An' that's where you're headed?'

Harry nodded ruefully. 'I managed to get this far on the money my parents gave me. When that ran out, I got involved in that card game in order to boost my finances, and — well, you know the rest.'

Jake turned right and stepped through a doorway into a neat, plank-built tonsorial parlour. A big man with a blond-white beard was trimming hair at one of two fancy hinged chairs. He identified Jake in the mirror directly in front of him and offered a greeting.

''Lo, Jake.'

Because he was Norwegian, he made 'Jake' sound like 'Yake'.

'You have an argumen' with somebody's window?'

'Somethin' like that. Listen, Per. Me an' my buddy here crave to bathe. I'd also 'preciate it iffen you c'd launder these here duds for me while I'm soakin'.'

'Sure. No problem.'

Per Grønmark called for his boy, Oscar, to fill the tubs he had set up in a tent out back. Then he told his two battered customers to go on through, and they did.

Within the quarter-hour, Jake and Harry were folded into their respective tubs, backs bent and knees jutting up in front of them, while young Oscar Grønmark ferried buckets of steaming water in from the range out back and doused each man in turn. A stray, warm breeze ruffled the tent's canvas walls and stirred the rising steam into little, sky-bound spirals as they scrubbed at their punished flesh. In all it was a very relaxing time.

Partway through stripping down, Harry had commented on the rash of purple bruises which had come up across Jake's back. It was certainly true that his back felt awful tender. But now the warm water eased some of the pain and stiffness from the wrangler's muscles, and the gritty tan soap rinsed away the thick, treacle-like smell of spilled alcohol.

In between scrubbing and soaking, the two unlikely companions got to know each other a little better. Harry said he'd been studying to be a quantity surveyor, whatever in hell that might be, before he'd gone to see his first movie. After that he'd become such an admirer of what he called 'the kinematographic medium' that his parents had eventually been compelled to let him follow his dreams.

The young Englishman was a witty, good-natured soul, and a born story-teller. To his surprise, Jake found himself warming to him. Harry might be a bit of a greenhorn, but he'd come this far in one piece, and Jake suspected that the young limey might have more grit than most folks would've imagined.

Jake had known him for just about one whole hour when he finally reached a decision. For better or worse, he decided to play his hunch.

'Harry,' he said a minute or so after Oscar brought his freshly-laundered clothes back into the tent and left them in a pile on the chair just beside the entrance. 'Let me ask you somethin'.'

The warm water had brought some colour back to Harry's face. 'Certainly, old boy.'

'Can you ride?'

'Why of course! I knew some of my happiest times on pony-trekking holidays, when I was a child. Why?'

Jake paused before taking the plunge. He was still in two minds. But . . . That Harry could be trusted to keep a confidence was obvious. The kid had that stiff-upper-lip code of honour that was so peculiar to the British. That he was in need of some fast cash was also evident.

His time was his own, and he could sure use the experience that being Jake's second man would provide.

At last he decided to follow his instincts. "Cause I might be able to offer you a job — if you can keep your mouth shut, that is: an' you don't mind givin' up the next three days in return for two hundred dollars.'

★　★　★

Bernie Woolcott was right. By eight o'clock that evening, grey-black storm-heads began to gather on the horizon, big, indistinct, smudges that presaged the most almighty downpour.

As Jake and Harry quit Maggie's place and paused for a moment before heading for their meeting with Elliott Blaze, the one-time wrangler eyed the clouds with satisfaction. 'Happen it rains as hard as ol' Bernie says it will,' he remarked, hefting his thirty-pound California saddle and modest warbag into a better position on his shoulder, 'I doubt there'll be too many soldiers out patrollin' the Rio tonight. That should make it a sight easier for us when it comes to gettin' across with all them guns in tow.'

Harry frowned. 'The cavalry runs regular patrols along the river, does it?'

'Has to,' Jake replied as they began to walk towards the centre of town. 'What with one thing an' another — border jumpers, *bandidos*, guerrillas and gun-runners — they can't afford to do anythin' else.'

Harry shoved his hands into the pockets of his brown trousers. He'd changed out of his seersucker suit after bathing, and dressed in a clean white shirt, open at the neck, and a brown alpaca suit. He still wore his crushed-up straw hat though. Jake figured it must be a kind of keepsake, for surely no-one would wear such a tile through choice.

'I tell you, Jake, I just can't wait to get cracking with this business. The excitement of it, the adventure . . . it's positively electrifying.'

Jake shot him a sour look. He personally felt anything *but* electrified. Most likely it was the thought of doing ten to twenty in Leavenworth if they got caught that made him feel that way. 'Just don't forget what I told you,' he cautioned as they crossed the still-brisk roadway.

'I won't,' Harry responded. 'You're the . . . what was it? The top hand. If you say jump, I ask, 'how high?''

'That's right,' Jake said gravely. 'An' that way, you might just get back here in one piece to spend your pay.'

Earlier, Jake had left it that he and whomever he managed to enlist as his second man would meet Elliott Blaze at Elliott's storage shed, where the guns and ammunition were being stored. They would take a circuitous route to the shed, picking up the horses and mules Jake and Miguel had purchased that morning along the way, so that when they arrived, probably some time around nine, they could load up under cover of darkness and then make tracks.

They made their first stop at the livery barn where Miguel had paid for the horses. Jake quickly made arrangements for a used but still serviceable Visalia saddle to be purchased for Harry in Elliott's name. While the stableman showed Harry how to saddle up, Jake cinched his own rig tight in a series of quick well practiced movements, silent and preoccupied.

In the event, the clash he'd been expecting to have with Maggie never materialised. There'd hardly been any kind of an argument at all, in fact. He'd just gone straight from home from Per Grønmark's barbershop, let himself in and shuffled through the house to the kitchen, where she was busy at the copper-lined sink, rinsing some carrots she'd just peeled and diced.

She'd been humming something low under her breath, caught up in her work. At first she didn't hear him pause there in the doorway. Then she somehow sensed him standing there watching her, and finally turned to look at him. Her full, handsome figure was encased in a blue calico dress that was slowly getting too tight for her. Some of her blonde curls and ringlets had been brushed back from her slightly-flushed face.

She looked at him wordlessly for a moment. Then she saw all the little pale glass-cuts beneath his eyes and on his cheeks and she just said, 'You been fighting.'

Like a kid about to be disciplined, he shifted his line of vision to the little pile of vegetables she'd been preparing. He nodded and said, 'Uh-huh,' because it was somehow easier to say that than to come right out and admit, 'Yeah, I have.'

She didn't say anything else, made no comments, asked no questions, so he cleared his throat and said, 'Listen. About that job of Elliott's . . . '

'You're taking it,' she said, dicing another carrot. 'Whatever it is.'

'Yeah, I'm takin' it.' He paused. 'I'll be away for a couple of days. Not too long. An' when I get back — '

'You won't be wanting an evening meal, then?' she cut in.

The question threw him for a moment. Then he shook his head. 'No.'

She glanced at him once, quickly, and he saw disappointment in her blue eyes.

He'd let her down, he knew that. Not by passing up on the evening meal, but by throwing in with Elliott. He'd let her down, and she was making him feel lousy about it.

'I'll be back in four, five days,' he told her.

She took no notice of him, just brushed past and went into the parlour. He followed her through the house, beginning to feel irritated by her behaviour.

'Mags — '

She pulled up sharp and spun to face him. 'Don't say another word about it, Jake! I don't want to know, all right? Whatever it is Elliott wants you to do, I don't want to know anything about it.'

He nodded. 'Don't then,' he said, harsher than intended.

Hurt washed across her face, mingling with the disappointment. Suddenly she wanted to get away from him and tried to hurry past, heading for the bedroom. He caught her arm and she tried to yank it free, but only succeeded in giving herself a Chinese burn.

'Dammit, Mags! What's the matter

with you? Look: the feller's offered me a job of work, an' you won't believe the pay! Why, a man'd have to be crazy to pass it up!'

She looked up at him. 'Oh? And just what have you got to do to earn all this money?'

He paused. 'Deliver somethin' to a feller across the line. Me an' another guy. Nothin' risky, I promise. Just a simple, straightforward delivery job.'

Her face betrayed nothing. At last she asked, 'What is it you'll be delivering?'

Quietly he said, 'Guns.'

She made a sound of anger in her throat then, and said, 'Oh, Jake — '

'Look, it's not as crooked as it sounds.'

'No?'

'No. President Wilson hisself — '

She pulled out of his grip. 'Oh, leave it, Jake! I don't want to hear it!'

'Well, you're *gonna* hear it!' he snapped. 'So just button your lip an' listen!'

She slapped him, and told him never to use that tone of voice on her again, and he could tell by the look on her face that she regretted it at once, just as he did, too.

'Mags — '

There was a noise over at the front door, and Harry stepped into the house, hefting his overstuffed suitcase in one hand. Raising his boater, he addressed Maggie. 'Uh . . . excuse me, dear lady . . . '

Maggie frowned. 'Who — ?'

'This is my partner,' Jake cut in. 'The other feller I was tellin' you about.'

Harry smiled at Maggie and said, 'I didn't mean to interrupt. It's just that, while I was waiting outside, I began to wonder if I might prevail upon you to look after all my personal effects here for the duration of our little jaunt down into Mexico?'

Maggie's frown deepened as she tried to decipher whatever it was the newcomer had just said. Finally she said, 'Ah, well . . . sure. I guess. But . . . don't take this personal mister, but . . . you're not from around these parts, are you?'

★　★　★

Elliott Blaze's storage shed was a small, thick-walled adobe that was no different to any of the other squat, white-washed shanties built in a wavering line down on the unclaimed land that fronted the river. Elliott and his prissy Mexican manservant, Miguel, were sitting in Elliott's Pope Hartford touring car right out front, waiting for Jake to arrive.

They didn't have to wait long. Jake and his second man arrived, leading fifteen long-eared mules in a long, nose-to-tail string, just before nine o'clock. While Miguel hurriedly climbed out of the auto to open Elliott's door for him, Jake and Harry swung down from their horses. Jake performed the introductions, and much to Elliott's surprise, Harry took his hand and pumped it energetically and said as how he was really looking forward to participating in this absolutely topping enterprise.

Before Elliott could say it, Jake intervened. 'No,' he said in a low voice. 'He's not from around these parts.'

Judging by the expression on his face, Elliott obviously had his doubts about the fresh-faced young man. 'Are you sure you're the right candidate for this business?' he asked bluntly.

'He's keen,' Jake cut in before Harry only made the matter worse. 'He c'n ride. He knows how to keep his mouth shut. An' I trust 'im.'

Elliott fingered his pencil moustache. 'Well . . . all right. If you're certain, Jake. But remember: I wouldn't take it kindly if anything went wrong — '

'Neither would I,' Jake growled, feeling edgy. 'Now — are we loadin' up your blessed guns, Elliott, or are we standin' around waitin' to be caught?'

Elliott eyed him sharply, but bit back a retort. 'We're loading the guns,' he replied.

It didn't take long, once Miguel had released all the padlocks on the shed door. Miguel and Harry did all the heavy lifting, Jake all the packing. Elliott just stood to one side, keeping watch.

There was a wide swathe of cleared ground directly ahead of the shed, stubbled with ocotillo and greasebrush. About seventy yards away stood a line of honky-tonks and bawdy-houses. Odd snatches of music and laughter drifted to them from over there, though not much light.

They worked hurriedly, in a silence broken only by heavy, tense breathing, beneath starlight. At last Jake checked all the loads one final time and announced that they were ready to go.

'Where will you ford the river?' Elliott asked.

They all knew that crossing the bridge that linked El Paso and Ciudad Juarez was out of the question.

'There's a bend about two, three miles southeast,' Jake replied. 'Water runs shallow there.'

Elliott nodded, oiled hair glistening faintly in the darkness. 'All right.' He reached into his overcoat pocket and brought out a handgun. 'Here, take it, Jake. You never know, you might need it.'

'What is it?'

'It's Colt, Model 1911 A1.'

Jake shook his head. 'Looks kind of new-fangled to me. Give it to the kid. I'll stick with the iron I brought with me.'

Elliott said to Harry, 'Can you be trusted not to blow your foot off with this?'

'Of course,' Harry replied stiffly.

Jake reached into his warbag and pulled out a coiled weapons belt with a beat-up old Peacemaker snuggled into the holster. Wordlessly he buckled the belt high around his waist, the first time he'd worn the thing in more than a decade at least. Then he said, 'Come on, then, Harry. We got a mess o' travellin' to do afore sun-up.'

Before he mounted up, Elliott offered his hand, and after a moment of surprise, Jake reached out to take it. As they shook, the first rumblings of thunder growled ominously in the distance, sounding like cannon-fire.

4

Harry led the mule-string southeast at a trot, following the winding contours of the Rio Grande, while Jake rode his blood-bay horse out ahead to keep a watch for cavalry patrols. In the northerly distance, the heavy purple clouds formed even greater bruises against the night sky, and a cool, blustery wind sprang up, pushing them further south. Soon the lights of El Paso began to fade in the northwest, and the only sounds were the constant drumming of horse- and mule-hooves, and the odd crack or rumble of thunder.

Forked lightning began to stilt-walk across the sky. Harry's piebald high-stepped a little, tossing its head nervously, and gradually its disquiet began to spread back along the string of mules.

After about thirty minutes, Jake rode back down the uneven, brush-littered trail towards him. He drew the blood-bay around to trot alongside the young Englishman and said, 'Seems all quiet up ahead.' He indicated the mules with a tilt of the jaw. 'How're they handlin'?'

'Skittish,' Harry replied, concentrating on his riding.

'Well, keep 'em on a firm rein, and don't let 'em forget who's boss.'

'All right.'

'Oh, an' one other thing . . . '

'Yes?'

Jake's face was sombre beneath the brim of his black Stetson. 'If we *do* happen to run into a cavalry patrol, jus' forget about the damn' mules an' make a run for it. Got that? Don't make things worse by tryin' to use that cannon Elliott gave you.'

His voice dropped a notch lower. 'Remember, Harry: them soldiers might be the enemy right now, but they're still Americans. Try throwin' lead at 'em an' I'll shoot you myself.'

Harry's lips tightened a fraction. 'You don't have to worry about me,' he said soberly.

'Good.'

They continued on, still trending southeast, in silence. To the north, the country opened out into a series of rolling, timber-topped hills. To the south, between Jake's small column and the river, rose a horse-high jumble of thorny chaparral: cholla, mesquite, yucca and manzanita shrubs.

It would be hell in there for a horse and his rider. They'd go in whole and come out the other side cut to bloody ribbons. But Jake was hoping to come upon a break in the natural barrier before too long, where goats had chewed a path through the wall of barbs and spikes.

The storm pushed closer. Lightning flared whitely, illuminating the grassy swells to the north. Thunder knocked and rattled up above. Within a minute, maybe two, fat raindrops started tapping against men and animals, softly at first, then gathering force and becoming more insistent.

Jake hauled his bright yellow slicker from where he'd rolled and buckled it behind his cantle, and quickly shrugged into it. 'You got somethin' to keep this rain off?' he asked.

Harry nodded. 'I've a lovely raincoat,' he said proudly. 'Personally tailored for me in Savile Row.'

'Did you think to bring it with you?'

The Englishman's expression turned sour. 'No. It's still in my suitcase, back at your good lady's place.'

'Well, if we're lucky, we'll be across the Rio before long. Then maybe we can find a place to fort up 'til this cloudburst passes over. Last thing we need right now is for you to catch pneumonia.'

Jake turned his attention to the sky, brown eyes blinking as the heavens wept right into his upturned face. The rain was growing steadily heavier, which was both good news — and bad. On the one hand, as he had noted earlier, a storm might keep the nightly cavalry patrols down to a minimum. But too much rain would also make his shallow fording place burst its banks and become impossible to use as a crossing.

Even as he thought about it, the rain began to come down harder, suddenly cutting visibility by more than half.

Lightning veined the sky, throwing its brief, ghostly glare across a wall of slanting rain directly ahead of them.

A moment passed, and then thunder gave an accompanying roar. Harry's piebald sidestepped and slipped in the rapidly-softening earth. With effort the Englishman fought the animal back onto an even keel. His alpaca suit was already soaked through, and beads of rainwater stood out on his cheeks and along his bruised jaw.

Jake hipped around in his saddle. This storm was spooking the mules, too. Their ears were up and their eyes were everywhere. Ahead, the trail was quickly becoming a swamp. Above, the rain showed no signs of slackening.

'Where . . . ?'

Jake turned back to his companion, yelling to make himself heard above another clatter of thunder. 'What was that?'

Harry also raised his voice. 'Where's this blessed path of yours, Jake? We haven't gone past it, have we?'

Jake looked around, trying to pierce the

sheeting rain in order to pick out a landmark from which to draw his bearings. At last he said, 'No, we're all right! It's about another half-mile straight ahead!'

Harry nodded, running a palm along his horse's neck. Jake went back along the line, muttering nonsense to the mules to keep them from panicking altogether. Elliott's crates were safely concealed beneath tarpaulins, so there was no danger of rainwater seeping through to damage the mechanisms of the weapons. Harry, though, he was a different matter. The poor feller was already drenched.

Lightning blazed. Thunder cracked viciously. Without warning Jake's blood-bay nickered and reared up, pawing at the damp air with its fore-hooves. It came back down with enough force to jar every bone in Jake's body, and he groaned and clenched his teeth against the pain.

Then he realised that the storm was passing over at last, heading into Mexico, and that the rain was easing up. He sagged a little as some of the tension ebbed out of him. As he spurred back down the line towards Harry, the rain lessened still further, so that its sharp, constant hiss was replaced by a softer, moist whisper.

Raindrops dripped from Jake's hat-brim. His horse and that of his companion began to relax and get back into stride.

'My goodness!' Harry said when Jake was near enough. 'And they complain about the British weather!'

'Come sun-up and it'll be as if that little downpour'd never happened,' Jake replied. 'It's dry country we're heading for, Harry. Bone dry, and hot as hell.' He straightened his back to ease some of the aches congregated there. 'Take my word for it: couple hours from now an' there won't even be so much as a puddle left.'

The last of the rain passed over, leaving the border country quiet save for the sounds of the men and their animals moving on through the gloom. One final cloud slipped away from the moon and the undulating countryside was suddenly transformed into a landscape of stark blacks and whites.

Five minutes passed before Harry muttered, 'Oh, no!'

Jake, who'd taken to brooding over Maggie again, threw him a look. 'Eh? What's up?'

'That wretched storm,' Harry replied. 'Can't you hear it? It's coming back!'

Jake listened. There was indeed a faint rumbling in the distance. But when he finally pinpointed the direction from which the sound was coming, it was to the north, not the south. He twisted around sharply, making his oilskin slicker crackle, and squinted off into the darkness.

Just coming out from behind a stand of timber that crowned a hill about a hundred yards away was a line of riders who'd most likely forted up beneath the arbour until the storm had passed over. He recognized their distinctive Montana peak hats at once, as well as the colour of their khaki uniforms, and cursed.

'Dammit! A patrol!'

Harry stiffened in his Visalia saddle. 'Do we run for it?' he asked tensely.

Jake replied without taking his eyes off

the far riders. 'No . . . leastways, not yet. I don't think they've spotted us yet.'

Harry took scant comfort from that. 'Then what shall we do?'

Jake thought fast, cursing himself for being too old, both mentally and physically, for all of this anxiety. Frantically he glanced around. The trail, and that gentle, grassy slope leading up to the soldiers, were both as bald as an egg. There was no cover at all except for the chaparral to the south, and that was practically impenetrable.

There was no option, then.

'Just keep goin',' Jake growled at last. 'An' pray they don't see us.'

But it was already way too late for prayer. One of the men in that twelve-man patrol suddenly yelled something and started pointing down toward the trail. Harry said, 'Cripes! That's torn it!'

Indeed it had. Jake cursed some more as the patrol began to swing around in their direction, and shift from a trot to a canter. He was just about to tell Harry to forget the deal, to leave the mules where they were and high-tail it before the soldiers could catch them, when he spotted the break in the chaparral they'd been aiming for.

At once a sharp surge of relief lightened his mood, although they were still a long way from being home and dry yet. '*There!*' he yelled to Harry, stabbing a finger at the break, which was only about a dozen feet away. 'That's the track I told you about!'

Harry spotted it. Up on the slope, there was some more shouting, and the pounding of hoofbeats coming closer.

'What are we waiting for, then?'

Jake said, 'Nothin'! Take the mules. I'll bring up the rear.'

Reaching a sudden, desperate decision, he tore his slicker open and hauled out his Peacemaker. Harry's eyes widened as he saw moonlight spill off the handgun's blued barrel.

'Jake! I thought you said — '

'I'll be aimin' high,' Jake replied tightly. 'Shootin' *over* 'em, not *at* 'em. Not that they're gonna know that. Now get goin'! An' for God's sake watch yourself on all them barbs!'

Harry heeled his piebald in the ribs and the horse, still a little spooked by the recent storm, took off like a stone from a catapult. The tie-line fastened around Harry's saddlehorn grew taut, then slackened a little as the mules behind him also began to gather speed.

Jake reined in his horse. The blood-bay pranced a little, hooves splashing in the moist, muddy earth, and turned to face the soldiers, who were still a good couple-hundred yards away.

He cast a brief glance at the pack-mules, just as the last one in line disappeared through the break in the thicket. It was going to be one hell of a ride for Harry Stanford-Brown, he thought. Even taking it nice and easy, a man would pick up cuts and tears from the brush hemming him in on both sides of the goat track. Trying to negotiate it at speed would cause considerably more damage to man and beast alike.

'*You, there! Stay right where you are!*'

Jake snapped his attention back to the oncoming soldiers, praying that Harry's horse wouldn't stumble and throw him, or that the mules wouldn't take a fall and add to all the confusion.

He listened for a moment to all the sounds the animals made crashing through the chaparral. That stretch of thorny brush was about a hundred yards wide, but once a man was beyond it, he had easy access to the Rio, and could cross it without too much difficulty, and with absolutely no witnesses.

Sucking in a sharp breath, he brought the old Peacemaker up on the knot of hard-riding men. He couldn't remember the last time he'd used the .45. Maybe he never had, except possibly up-ended, as a makeshift hammer. He raised the barrel slightly, thumbed back the hammer and very deliberately pulled the trigger.

The gun-blast tore through the night with a high, spiteful crack, and a spurt of bright yellow flame lanced from the barrel. Jake's horse sidestepped some more, but when he told it to stand still, it did.

Up on the slope, the non-com leading the patrol raised a hand and the column came to an untidy halt. There followed a moment of much animation as the soldiers began to haul their Springfields from leather.

Jake didn't want to give them that much time, though. Once they had weapons in their hands, they'd start shooting back at him, and he very much doubted that *they'd* be aiming high.

He fired another shot to keep them occupied, and saw their horses mill around a little, uncertain as to just what was happening. He sent a third slug into the darkness, just to let them know he meant business, and that they shouldn't try coming any closer, and this time he was rewarded with some more shouting as the soldiers fought to control their nervous mounts.

He'd been trying to keep track of Harry's progress in his mind. Barring accidents, the young Englishman should be well on his way by now. He brought the Peacemaker up one more time and pulled the trigger again.

Nothing happened.

Thumbing back the hammer, he tried again.

Nothing.

He swore. He knew the weapon was fully loaded. He'd loaded it himself, just this afternoon. Why, against his better judgment he'd even slipped a cartridge into the sixth chamber, which most sensible men tended to leave empty, for the hammer to rest on.

Still, this was no time to ponder the whys and wherefores of it. All that mattered was that the damn' gun, or perhaps the admittedly-old shells with which he'd loaded it, had ceased to function.

The deep, unsociable roar of a carbine cut across the night. At least one of the soldiers had managed to get his saddle-gun out and working, then.

Again Jake's horse started tossing its head and prancing through the mud. Somewhere a .45/.70 slug chopped into the spiky tangle behind him. Another shot followed quickly on its heels, another, another and one more.

The blood-bay started acting up even more. Jake jammed the Colt back into its holster. He had no other weapon worth mention. Few range men ever carried long guns attached to their rigs, for fear that their reins or lariats would snag on them, and Jake was no exception.

That only left one option; flight.

Again he loosed an oath. He'd hoped to buy them a little more time before disappearing into the chaparral himself, but there was no help for it now. Another bullet tore into the leafy backdrop. If he stuck around much longer, the soldiers would eventually find their range.

That decided him.

Kicking the blood-bay in the ribs, he turned the animal on a dime and sent it racing for the goat track. With any luck, the soldiers might be wary about following him, in case he decided to lay in wait for them.

The horse entered the chaparral at a flat-out gallop and Jake quickly shoved all other considerations aside in order to concentrate on his riding.

The goats had done admirable work clearing a path through all the inhospitable vegetation, but it was a pretty narrow thoroughfare all the same, and given to all kinds of twists and turns that made the negotiation of it even more hazardous.

Jake leaned forward across his horse's flying mane, hoping to God that he wouldn't lose one of his eyes to any of that lethal-looking foliage overhanging the path. The blood-bay swerved this way and that, its great lungs heaving. Every so often it stumbled, momentarily distracted by the pain of a scratch or a gouge, but somehow it always managed to find its footing again.

For his part, Jake didn't fare quite so badly, mainly due to the heavy slicker he still wore. Even so, he caught some minor scratches to his already tender face and knuckles, a couple of them deep and ragged enough to draw blood.

His flight through the brush seemed to last forever. Half the time he was riding blind, with his eyes screwed shut. He took a few more cuts on the backs of his hands, and once the blood-bay nearly lost its balance altogether and crashed against one of the thicket-walls with a high, womanish scream.

Then the thorny tangle started to thin, and almost before he knew it, the horse was crashing through the last of it, eyes showing their whites in fear, big mouth flecked with foam.

Jake hauled back on the reins and the blood-bay skidded to a stiff-legged halt that sprayed mud and sand everywhere. Jake nearly fell from the saddle, gulping for air as hard and as fast as his mount.

'Jake! Thank heavens!'

He snapped his head toward the voice. Harry was sitting his mount about fifteen feet away, with the pack-mules strung out behind him. He was still mopping at the facial cuts he'd sustained during his own mad rush through the chaparral.

'When all that shooting started — '

Jake just shook his head. There was no time for any of that now. Already he thought he could hear the distant, crashing sounds of pursuit.

'Just get goin'!' he gasped, waving a palm towards the river's edge. 'Quickly now!'

Harry bobbed his head, shoved his handkerchief into his jacket pocket and urged his piebald back into motion. The horse headed for the water at a trot. Still jumpy, it was glad to be moving again.

The mules followed behind in mincing little steps. Jake watched them go, heading for the oily black water and the liquid reflections of the stars it contained. Suddenly he heard a noise someplace behind him and threw a look over his shoulder.

There!

It wasn't his imagination, then: judging by the sounds coming from within the chaparral now, the soldiers were coming straight after him.

'Hurry it up, there!' he hissed urgently.

Harry glanced back over his shoulder. His horse was only fetlock-deep in the Rio's chilly water. 'I'm going as fast as I dare!'

Jake regretted not having asked the Englishman for his Colt 1911 A1. If he could have discharged a few more rounds into the sky, it might have discouraged their pursuers a bit. Chances were, though, that he wouldn't have known how to operate the automatic pistol, anyway.

At last Harry was about midway across the river, with the mules splashing along behind him. The water had risen as far as his piebald's belly, then levelled out.

There was a yell from inside the tangle of chaparral. Jake felt a sudden, irrational sense of satisfaction. Whoever was leading the patrol through the undergrowth — more than likely the non-com — was picking up more cuts than he'd bargained for.

But the sound of single-file cavalry mounts crashing headlong through the brush was getting steadily closer. Jake knew he daren't hang around any longer. He said, 'Yah!' and sent his horse racing for the water's edge.

Man and mount entered the Rio, with disturbed water boiling all around them. Jake angled the blood-bay up alongside the mules, and yelled at them to get a move on.

The far bank lay about forty or fifty yards away. The blood-bay was unsure of its footing. Jake, knowing that the river-bottom along this stretch was passably flat, urged the high-stepping animal on.

Harry's mount came up on the far side of the river, glistening wetly in the moonlight, and spraying water from its sleek coat like droplets of molten silver. The Englishman reined in and hipped around, but Jake waved him on.

'*Keep movin'!*'

To his credit, Harry wasted no time in questioning him about it, just did what he'd been told, aiming for the cover of some scrub fringing the rim of the slight, shelving gradient that led away from the river-bank.

The first of the pursuing soldiers burst out of the chaparral just about then. Jake heard the noise he made barging into the open and quickly chanced a look over his shoulder.

It was the non-com, all right, with a battered, angry face, a once-neat khaki uniform that the foliage had shredded, and glittering eyes that glared daggers at him.

'*Hold it, whoever you are! In the name o' the United States Army!*'

Jake paid him no heed, just kept his horse ploughing through the water towards the far bank.

A gunshot cracked through the night air. Jake thought he felt the wind of the bullet whistle past his ear, but maybe that was only his imagination.

Another soldier broke out of the chaparral. The non-com raised his hand-gun and fired a second shot. Silently, bending low, Jake thanked his lucky stars that the sergeant was a lousy shot: either that, or that the moonlight was severely hampering his aim.

The river-bottom angled upwards beneath his blood-bay's pumping legs. Suddenly the water level began to fall. The horse came up on the far bank and picked up speed almost at once, taking the brushy slope at a fast run.

A couple more shots followed Jake as he went through all that scrub and cactus and joined his companion and the pack-mules on the other side of the ridge. Harry was shivering, he saw as he reined in beside him, but with a mixture of cold and excitement, not fear.

'Are you all right?' the Englishman asked with genuine concern.

Jake nodded, too breathless to answer him any other way.

'Will they come for us?' Harry prompted, keeping his blue eyes on the ridge, beyond which all had now fallen quiet.

Jake shook his head. 'I doubt it,' he said at last. 'Not lessen they want to start an international incident, anyway.'

His uncharacteristic smile was filled with relief, but short-lived all the same. 'Come on, Harry,' he said. 'We've made it this far, at least. But let's get the hell out of here now. All that shootin's bound to bring the *rurales* a-runnin', an' I'd as soon avoid tanglin' with those damned Mexican policemen if I can help it.'

★   ★   ★

They rode on through the night, and even though they'd bedded down in Maggie's parlour for most of the afternoon, the following sunrise still found them glassy-eyed and bone weary.

Jake rode point, keeping watch for trouble. Harry followed on, leading the string of mules behind him. Around them the flat, arid land was silent and still. Away to the south, many miles distant, rose craggy purple mountains. Between that high country and their present position, the landscape was filled from one horizon to the other with an unending field of sagebrush.

Dawn bleached some of the charcoal from the sky, leaving it grey at first, then white, then amber, then blue. As the climbing sun rose higher, some of the night-time cold left the land, and the warmth — still bearable at this early hour — livened the two men up a little.

Right from the start, Jake had elected to travel by night and rest up during the day. For one thing, the heat, which would build to furnace-level by noon, would soon wear both men and animals down. For another, these were dangerous parts. Jake hoped that there'd be less chance of running into trouble if they moved under cover of darkness.

They were to deliver Elliott's guns to a place called Los Caballos Mestenos, which lay some seventy miles to the south. They had been given three days in which to do it. Jake saw no problems there, provided they were careful. Within four days they could be heading back home, the job behind them.

The morning began to grow old. Jake glanced back once and saw Harry dozing in the saddle. He returned his watchful gaze to their surroundings. The land was being carved up now by arroyos and barrancas. Away to the east, the terrain rose up in a series of weathered sandstone bluffs.

Jake considered the high ground to be the best place to make camp. From the position of the sun he estimated the time to be approaching eight-thirty or nine. They'd been in the saddle for a dozen hours or thereabouts. Now he figured that enough was enough.

He dropped back, reached over and shook Harry awake. 'Come on, kid. We'll fort up for the day in those rocks yonder.'

Harry squinted at the high ground, then nodded. 'All right.' He sounded as tired as he looked, and looked ragged now that the chaparral had torn his fancy alpaca suit to tatters.

They followed an old, overgrown track toward the bluffs. Saguarro and cholla hemmed them in on both sides. Gradually the ground beneath them — still as hard as diamonds in spite of the rain, as Jake had said — began to rise. They followed it higher until they came to a sizeable patch of land that held enough scrubby grass for the animals to graze on, and man-high rocks on three sides, which would hide their presence from anyone down on the flats.

Both men came down out of their saddles with grateful, exhausted sighs. There'd been a time when Jake could stay aboard a horse from dawn 'til dusk and never complain about it. But he'd been younger then. Now all he wanted was rest. Rest and coffee and some food to fill his belly.

He asked Harry if he knew how to cook. Harry said he didn't, but that he could soon learn. Jake told him to break out the skillet Miguel had packed away for them, and see what he could rustle up. Then, leaving the younger man to it, he busied himself unloading the mules and then taking care of the horses.

He worked quietly and methodically, with a horseman's consideration for his mount. He upended their saddles off to one side and draped their saddle-blankets on a rock, sweat-side up, to dry out. Then he checked the horses' backs for any signs of saddle-sores, and finding none, turned his attention to their legs. Finally he went to fetch an old jar of liniment he'd always carried in his warbag, and treated the cuts the animals had sustained in the chaparral before watering, then feeding them.

By the time he was through, Harry had found some dead brush and started a small fire, over which he was frying beans and boiling coffee.

The entire scene was all very peaceful.

And then pistols started blasting in the distance.

5

Twenty-four hours earlier, Harry would have had to ask what that sudden, violent fusillade was. Now he recognised it at once.

'Ruddy hell, Jake! Gunfire!'

It was hard to pinpoint the direction from which it was coming with any degree of accuracy. These open flatlands had a way of distorting sound, and tying it up with misleading echoes.

Jake had a pretty fair idea, though. Unless he was much mistaken, it was coming from the south and east — and not too far southeast, either.

He and Harry came up off the ground and Jake told the Englishman to put out the fire before any smoke it might give off could betray their position. While Harry set the skillet and coffee pot aside and kicked sand over the little blaze, Jake's right hand instinctively dropped to his Peacemaker. He cursed, remembering how the wretched thing had let him down the previous night, then held his hand out to his companion, flexing his long fingers urgently. 'Quick! Let's have Elliott's automatic over here.'

Harry drew the pistol from his waistband and passed it over, butt-first. It was an odd weapon, Jake thought, all straight lines and angles, and alien in his grip. Still, a gun was a gun, and talking of guns . . .

Someone beyond the seamed grey rocks fringing the south side of their little camp was using up ammunition like it was going out of style, and Jake wanted to know who they were and why they were at it.

Over by the makeshift corral he'd created from their lariats, the horses and mules pricked up their ears and flared their nostrils. The animals watched him hustle over the far rocks, whip off his hat and climb high enough to take a look-see at what was going on. Within seconds Harry was clambering up to join him at his impromptu watchtower.

'What is it, Jake? What's going on?'

Jake made no reply. By now the kid was in position to see for himself.

About half a mile away, a patrol of *rurales* just coming out of a steep-sided canyon by way of a brush-littered draw had been ambushed by an indeterminate number of bandits. The bandits, it appeared, had timed their attack perfectly.

As they fired down at the rural policemen from both sides of the gully, it was obvious that they'd caught their victims completely flatfooted. Even as they watched, Jake and Harry saw uniformed men topple from rearing mounts, grabbing at wounds in their chests, shoulders or heads. *Rurales* landed hard in the boiling dust, bloodied, wounded or dead.

In no way could Jake call what he was witnessing a fight, because it wasn't. It was a slaughter, plain and simple.

Beside him, Harry swallowed hard. 'Can't we do something to stop this, Jake?'

Jake shook his head.

'But . . . those policemen, they're being

massacred! We can't just stand aside and watch it happen!'

'We can,' Jake replied grimly. 'An' lessen you want to bring them *bandidos* up here after us, we *will*.'

Harry fell silent. In a morbid, nauseating way the ambush held him fascinated. But it didn't last long. How long could it take to shoot a dozen rats in a barrel? Pretty soon there was nothing left standing down there in that far, brush-littered draw except riderless horses.

Harry let out a long breath and shivered despite the heat.

If anything, the looting took a little longer than the killing. When they were certain they'd accounted for the entire patrol, the bandits came down off the slopes and set to work. As near as Jake and Harry could tell from this distance, they took everything: the horses, saddles and supplies, the dead men's weapons, money, uniforms and boots. For all the two unlikely gunrunners knew, they even pried the gold teeth out of the dead men's mouths.

It was an efficient, thorough job of

thievery, and, for the bandits, profitable too. When at last they were finished, a couple of them brought more horses over from beyond the south side of the draw and they all mounted up.

Jake's breath caught in his throat. If those bandits should come this way and spot them . . .

He expelled a long sigh when they twisted their horses away to the east, galloped up the slope and along the canyon rim before disappearing from sight beyond a jagged ridge.

Jake waited a while, until he was certain they wouldn't be coming back. Inside, his guts felt quivery. Up above, ragged-winged *zopilotes* began to circle over the now-still draw, sensing a feast. After a while the buzzards dropped lower toward the bodies, and he turned away fast, having no particular desire to see what happened next.

He climbed down from the rocks and Harry followed suit. Neither man had much of an appetite now, but they both craved coffee. Harry drank two cups in silence, still stunned by what he'd seen.

Jake was a bit more pragmatic. Whilst it had surely sickened him, the massacre of the *rurales* had also impressed upon him the need for adequate protection. Now he intended to see that they had it.

Handing the automatic back to the Englishman, he took his own Peacemaker from leather, flipped open the gate and emptied the weapon, inspecting the two bullets which had refused to fire. As he had suspected, they'd lain around for so long that the bases were mottled with rust. He tossed the shells away with disgust, and did the same with the rounds in his belt, which were about the same age.

'Harry, go fetch me a new box of .45s, will you? Keep some spares in your pockets for the automatic, too. From now on, we travel ready to fight.'

Harry nodded, hollow-eyed. 'Very well.'

'An' after that, bed down for a while. You look worn to a frazzle, boy.'

'I'll be all r — '

'Bed down,' Jake repeated firmly. 'I'll take first watch. You can spell me at one.'

As it turned out, there was no need for

such dramatic precautions. The surrounding desert remained empty and undisturbed the rest of the day. When Jake woke up later that afternoon, the pair of them ate the beans and finished off with a tin of sardines each. It was simple, crude fare, but Harry, who must have been used to a much grander diet, voiced no complaints.

The day had been murderously hot, even in the meagre shade, but at last, as evening approached, it cooled off a little. By the time full dark had descended, the horses were saddled and the mules re-packed. They were ready to move on.

The bloated moon shone down on them as they came out onto the flatland. Once again, Jake rode point and Harry took charge of the mule-train.

Unfortunately they had to ride through the corpse-cluttered draw and on into the south-trending canyon beyond in order to keep heading in the right direction for their destination. It was a chilling experience, and it spooked men and animals alike.

The dead *rurales* had been stripped

down to their trap-door combinations. They lay sprawled in various attitudes of death. Some had died straight away from their bullet wounds. Others, who hadn't been so lucky, had been dispatched with a knife across the throat. To one extent or another, all of them had provided food for the buzzards.

When the draw lay behind them, the travelling became easier. As the night wore on, the miles unwound beneath them. Once, Jake looked around to find Harry peering over his shoulder at their inky back-trail. 'You all right there, boy?'

Harry didn't answer at once. Then he turned back to face front again. 'Yes. I thought I heard a noise, that's all. As if someone were following us.'

Jake made no comment. It was likely that the kid was still thinking all about those poor dead sonsof-bitches they'd passed in the draw, and picturing all manner of ghoulish resurrections in his mind, as men often did when surrounded by a dark, silent night.

By dawn the following day, Jake estimated that they'd come between twelve and fifteen miles from their camp-site. They found another high place to fort up for the coming day. It was not as ideal as their original camp, but it would do. All around them, the desert stretched away dry and broken, all rock and sand, a place where only the hardiest of plants and animals could hope to survive.

Again Jake took the first watch, while Harry stretched out in rock-shade and slept. Already the heat was cloying. He watched the quivering distance, awed by the desolation of the land, and pleased, too. If possible he wanted to avoid even the smallest outpost of civilisation on his way to Los Caballos Mestenos. The fewer people who saw them, the less chance there was of trouble.

He thought about the near-miss they'd had with the soldiers up by the Rio, and the massacre they'd witnessed the day before. He realised that he was going to earn every nickel of his five hundred dollars.

Gradually the morning wore on and at midday Harry rolled out of his blankets and scratched vigorously at the stubble shading his lower face. 'How has it been, Jake?'

'Quiet.'

'Well, let's hope it stays that way.'

Jake checked on the animals one last time, then measured his length on the blanket and quickly fell asleep.

The afternoon passed slowly and without event. It got hotter, and then, as the sun began to sink, it started cooling off again. When Jake awoke, they ate a quick meal and washed it down with coffee.

'Better go steady on the water from here on in,' Jake decided as he limped over to his upended saddle and set about preparing the animals for the next leg of the journey. 'If you think we've passed through some pretty dry country already, you ain't seen nothin' yet.'

Harry only muttered, 'Hmmm.'

The night turned cold. It was a relief to keep moving. The desert was largely flat and without obstructions, so the pace was good. They rode in silence, except to curse the night-chill or urge the horses and mules ever onward.

At last the sky began to lighten slowly in the east. Jake almost hated to call a halt. By his reckoning, they'd covered eighteen or twenty miles, though gauging distance was often tricky by starlight.

Deciding to push on as long as he could, he busied himself with a few mental calculations. In total, he figured they'd covered nearly forty miles since crossing the Rio. If they could top the twenty-mile mark in tonight's stage of the trek, they ought to be able to chance the last ten or so miles to Los Caballos Mestenos tomorrow morning, and arrive bang on schedule.

For the first time in days, his spirits lifted.

They continued on toward the south. The sun rose higher and pushed the blood-bay's shadow off to the right. At last Jake's eyelids began to drop and he knew that Harry was probably feeling just as tired himself.

Spying a slope topped with Joshua trees and cottonwoods away to the east, he hipped around in the saddle and pointed.

Harry, who was leading the flagging mules about twenty feet behind, followed his gaze and gave a thumbs-up of understanding and agreement.

Jake led them off what passed for a trail in this wilderness and headed for the timber. It had been chancy bringing a greenhorn like Harry along on a job like this, he thought, but as it had turned out, the Englishman had been a good choice. He'd pulled his weight, he followed orders and best of all, he never complained.

They reached the edge of the timber and continued on toward its centre, where they would be concealed from anyone on the lower elevations, and protected from the hammering sun above. All around them, yellow-tipped brittle-bush and red-flowered barrel cactus studded the black, rocky terrain. There was a sickly splash of needle grass in among the trees which would just about provide forage for the animals, but other than that it was a deadening vista; hell without the flames.

When they reached a clearing just wide

enough for their needs, Jake reined in and cooled his saddle. Because of the injuries he'd sustained eighteen months earlier, and because he'd grown unused to riding ever since, his back, arms and legs ached something fierce.

Stretching, he allowed himself a jaw-cracking yawn. Harry led the mules into the clearing and also slipped wearily out of the saddle. Wordlessly he saw to the comfort of his piebald as Jake reached for one of the three water skins they'd been packing, which were draped across the lead mule.

The skin was loose and deflated.

With a frown, Jake shook it and listened to the sorry sound an inch or two of water made at the bottom of the container.

Panicking a little, for this was not exactly the best kind of country in which to run low on water, he reached across the mule and grabbed the second skin. That one made a similar, almost-empty sound.

The third skin made no splashing sounds at all.

Jake stood there for a moment, puzzled. They'd been careful with their water, right from the first. Jake had made sure of that. With a little forethought, the water in those skins should have lasted them three days, easily.

Quickly he checked the skins for holes. There were none. Evaporation, then? It was a possibility, of course, but a vague one.

'Anything the matter, old boy?'

He turned and found Harry watching him from the other side of the clearing. Jake returned his gaze, scratching thoughtfully at the whiskers sprouting from his chin.

'Water,' he replied. 'We got about two or three swallows left.' He shook the skins to prove it. 'I'm sure we — '

Suddenly he fell silent. His tired gaze sharpened on Harry. He dropped the skins to the ground and came closer, very slowly. When he was about three feet away he said, 'You *sonofabitch*.'

Harry looked decidedly uncomfortable. 'I don't know what — '

Jake reached out and grabbed him by

119

his tattered lapels, hauling him forward so that their faces were no more than five or six inches apart. 'You senseless sonofabitch!' he repeated, angrier now. 'You used the last of that water to wash in, didn't you? To wash and *shave*.'

There was nothing to be gained by denying it, even if Harry had been the type to lie or make excuses. His round face, shadowed with stubble the day before, was smoother than a baby's backside now. He said quietly, 'I didn't know it was the last of the water when I used it. It's just that my beard was getting so itchy — '

'Itchy!' Jake shoved the Englishman away from him, more angry than he could say. 'So what did you do? Wait 'til I was asleep before you set to with your razor?'

He was not a violent man, but he felt like hitting Harry right then, and that frightened him.

'Do you know what you've done? *Do* you? You've damn-near signed our death warrants, that's what you've done!'

He shuffled forward threateningly. 'You got any idea how long a man can survive out here without water?' He snapped his fingers. 'About *that* long, that's what! An' what about the mules? How long do you suppose they'll be able to keep goin'?' He shook his head in disgust, then spat off to one side. 'You stupid, thoughtless sonofabitch!'

Harry looked wretched. Clearing his throat, he said, 'I'm sorry.'

'*Sorry!*'

'Well . . . can't we dig for an underground spring or something? I mean, aren't there plants from which we could extract moisture? Until we find a water-hole?'

There were plants, but Jake was damned if he knew which ones, or how to set about extracting the water once he found them. He'd spent most of his life in land where water was, if not plentiful, at least relatively easy to get at.

'Of all the brainless . . . ' He let the sentence fade and spun away from the shame-faced limey, whipping his hat off and running splayed fingers through his short, dust-coloured hair, mussing up his centre parting.

He closed his gritty eyes, forcing himself to calm down. He felt tired and sore and yeah, thirsty too. But as annoyed as he was with Harry, he knew there was nothing to be gained by chewing him out any more. The kid had made a mistake, but Jake doubted that he would ever make the same one twice.

He steered his thoughts toward finding a way out of their predicament. They had to have water, no two ways about it. But dare they rely on finding a tinaja, or natural water tank, out here? Jake didn't think so. A man could die waiting to find the fluid he needed to survive in these parts.

He clapped his hat back on and stared through the trees to the sunglare beyond. Hoping to find water was too damn' risky. But heading for a place they knew full well could supply the stuff: well, that was different. Only trouble was, that meant aiming for civilisation — not that they really had much choice.

Without looking around, Jake said, 'You got that map Elliott gave us the night we quit El Paso?'

Harry was so anxious to please now that he almost tore the thing apart in his haste to get it out of his jacket pocket.

'Here.'

Jake took it and opened it out. He frowned at all the lines and contours for a long time, trying to pinpoint their approximate location. After a minute or so Harry said tentatively, 'Need any help, old boy?'

'No!'

'It's just that you — '

'Look, I don't need your help, dammit!'

Harry nodded. 'Very well. But if you're trying to ascertain our current whereabouts, we're just about . . . there.'

He pointed. Jake focused on the area his companion had indicated. The kid was right, although Jake refused to acknowledge the fact. Instead he began to search the surrounding terrain for a town, and found one about ten miles southwest of their present position, a little place by the looks of it, called Linosa.

He shoved the map back at Harry and said, 'Fold it.'

Then he eyed his tired blood-bay and

sighed heavily at the prospect of more riding. Still, there was no help for it. Lord knew, they wouldn't get far without water.

As the Englishman refolded the map, Jake limped over to the discarded water skins and bent to pick them up. He explained his intentions as he tied them to his saddlehorn.

'But . . . a twenty-mile round trip, Jake! In this heat! And all because of me!' Harry wrung his hands. 'Here, let me go instead.'

'Forget it.'

'But it's the least I can do!'

'You'd likely get lost an' cause more problems than we already got.'

Harry's blue eyes dropped away from Jake's seamed face, and his shoulders slumped. 'Yes,' he said in a quiet voice. 'You're probably right.'

That made Jake feel bad. He didn't want to dishearten the younger man. Moderating his tone, he said, 'Jus' see to the animals, kid, an' keep your eyes peeled, all right? I'll be back soon as I can.'

Harry bobbed his head. 'Leave it to me. I won't let you down again, Jake. My word on it.'

Suppressing a groan, Jake hauled himself back across leather and left the clearing behind him at a bone-rattling walk.

★　★　★

Linosa turned out to be what Jake's old bunkhouse buddies used to call just another wide place in the road, a cluster of white-washed adobes which had grown up in a passably verdant bowl of land where the main road from Ciudad Juarez to Chihuahua and Hidalgo del Parral dribbled in a more or less straight line south.

When Jake topped a rise to the southeast two hours later, he reined in amid a line of scrubby palo verde trees and eyed the place cautiously. Linosa boasted one street. A livery barn, a couple of cantinas and stores, a beanery and a schoolhouse were the only commercial buildings. The rest were mean-looking little dwelling-places, most of them in poor repair.

The town was reasonably busy, for it was early, and siesta-time still lay several hours in the future. Jake spied men and women going about their chores, all of them dressed in the ragged white pyjamas or all-concealing black dresses of the masses, a bunch of chickens squawking in the middle of the dusty road, a tethered goat trying to chew his way through the rope holding him captive and a couple of dogs sprawled out in shade.

From the schoolhouse came the sweet sounds of children singing a hymn. Jake's eyes lingered on the well midway down the single street. He knew that *gringos* were rare in Mexico these days, what with the trouble and all, and that his presence would probably arouse unwanted atten-tion, but he didn't figure to stick around any longer than it took to spell his horse, fill their skins and maybe wash his throat with a glass of tequila.

He nudged the blood-bay in the ribs. The horse was as tuckered as he was. It plodded stiff-legged down the incline and onto the main trail, flecked with sweat and dust, and stumbling a bit with weariness.

Jake expected to get some strange looks as he rode in, and the townsfolk didn't disappoint him. Men and women, be they old or young, all regarded him with suspicion, curiosity, fear and hatred. But then again, they were fearful and suspicious of most strangers in these unsettled parts. This was not a time for trust, after all, only caution.

The blood-bay smelled water in the air and sensed that they had reached their destination. Its pace quickened as they angled toward the public corrals, where the animal could be turned loose for a while to chew green grass and suck up clear, cool water.

Jake dismounted, smelling a hot chili dish in the still, muggy air. He felt hot and sticky, and he craved a bath to clean the salt from his pores, but knew this was neither the time nor the place for such a luxury.

Against his better judgement, he off-saddled the blood-bay and left his saddle and blanket hanging over the top rail of the corral, where other patrons had also left their gear. He watched while the horse drank its fill at the trough, shooing it away when he figured it had had enough, then surveyed the town from beneath his hat-trim, still aware of the sidelong glances he was receiving.

A moment later he headed for the plain stone well with the three empty skins slung across his shoulder. Away to the north, the road was empty of traffic. Southward, a couple of riders, *vaqueros* by the look of them, were leaving town at a canter. Jake stifled a yawn, sighed instead, and set to work filling the skins.

He was just capping the first, and getting ready to start replenishing the second, when a voice somewhere behind him called out, 'Goin' on a long journey, my friend?'

The short hairs at the nape of Jake's neck stirred uncomfortably. He suddenly became aware of a peculiar silence in the street, an emptiness, too. He stopped what he was doing and turned around slowly to confirm his worst suspicions.

Two men were lounging outside one of the cantinas, no more than thirty feet away. Their uniforms — buff-coloured shirts beneath olive green vests, and distinctive *charro* sombreros the colour of chocolate — identified them beyond all doubt as *federales*: Government troops.

One of them was a corporal, the other a sergeant. The sergeant was about forty, older than his companion by a dozen years. Both had dark, mottled skins, hooded eyes and the look and manner of bullies. The corporal, tall, slim and confident, was obviously a ladies' man. The sergeant was bigger, blunt-featured, with spade-sized hands and a twisted, ugly mouth. The corporal had asked the question.

Jake tried to ignore the heavy ball of dread which settled in his stomach. He put a smile on his face, but had the feeling that it looked awful sick. 'Well, you know. This is dry country. Pays to have more'n you think you'll need.'

The corporal nodded. '*Si, naturalmente*. But you haven't answered my question.'

He pushed up off the abobe wall and tucked his thumbs into the weapons belt buckled around his narrow hips. There was no doubt that he would use his gun if an answer was not forthcoming. 'Goin' far?'

Not for the first time, Jake cursed his luck. Under any other circumstances, the *federales* wouldn't have given him a second glance. But these were not other circumstances, and while he was stove-up, getting along in years and in no way remarkable, it could be that the enemies of the state — people like Villa, Zapata or Carranza — had chosen him for some subversive task for exactly that reason.

'Not far,' he replied at last. 'Hidalgo del Parral, maybe. I hear they got some sweet country down that way. Heard that some of the cattle spreads there might be hirin' on.'

It was a pretty thin story, but there'd been no time to concoct anything more elaborate.

The *federales* saw through it right away, he could tell. The sergeant came up off the wall too, and his rough-skinned left hand came oh-so-close to the butt of his fancy French handgun.

'Bit old for range-work, aren't you, *abuelo?*' said the corporal, slowly closing the distance between them. The street was practically empty now. Only the squawking chickens remained, oblivious to the tension electrifying the humid morning air.

'I been breakin' horses all my life,' Jake heard himself reply. 'Figure there's always work for a man who knows his trade. An' by the way, son: I'm *not* your gran'paw.'

'Then what is your name?'

Jake said the first thing that came into his mind. 'Harry Brown.'

'You have proof of that? Documents of some kind?'

He swallowed. 'No.'

The corporal's expression changed minutely. He'd reached a decision about Jake. His eyes took on a hard, spiteful quality. 'What is your business here in Mexico, *señor?* Your *real* business?'

Jake knew there was nothing to gain by spinning any more yarns. These bean-eating buckos had already figured that he was up to something. But what were they aiming to do about it? *Arrest* him? Most likely.

Frantically he tried again, hoping to God that his nerve wouldn't betray him. 'I jus' told you what my business is, corporal. What's this all about, anyway? It's not a crime to fill a couple skins with water, is it?'

The corporal shook his head. 'No,' he replied. 'But it *is* a crime to run guns across the Rio, *señor*. And according to intelligence we've received from your United States Army, that is exactly what someone did three nights ago.'

Jake was a lousy liar. He could feel the blood leaving his skin, and he wouldn't meet the corporal's gaze. But still he tried manfully. 'What? An' you think that was *me?*'

'I don't know. But I think we'll take you in for questioning, anyway. Just in case.'

Jake knew then that he was sunk. Even supposing he could convince these *federales* that they were mistaken — a forlorn hope at best — he couldn't spare the time it would take. So, as he'd told Stinky Bill Anderson a lifetime before, it was time to *shut* up, or *put* up.

And just like ol' Stinky Bill, Jake chose to put up.

6

Desperate situations call for desperate measures, and Jake was feeling pretty desperate just then.

With his guts screwed tight enough to burst at the seams, he threw the water skin he'd just filled at the corporal, and while the movement diverted the attention of the *federales* away from him, he reached down and whipped out his Peacemaker.

'All right, you two! Hands up!'

Although he sounded tougher than a boiled owl, he guessed he must look pretty comical standing there like an old-time badman, because the blunt-featured sergeant didn't put his hands up at all, he just gave a little chuckle and said, 'Put that antique down, *abuelo*, and maybe we'll overlook your stupidity when we write our reports.'

Jake kept his eyes shuttling back and forth between them. His heart was hammering so hard that he felt a little sick. For the first time he wondered if these two soldiers were in town alone, or whether they had some more men with them.

'Put your hands up, I said!' Jake snapped. 'I mean it!'

'No you don't,' the corporal said in a persuasive voice. Behind him, the sergeant was evidently inclined to agree, because far from raising his hands, he began to yank out his sidearm.

Jake reacted instinctively. Tilting the Peacemaker's barrel a fraction, he fired the gun, silently praying that the weapon wouldn't let him down as it had that night by the Rio.

It didn't. The gun bucked in his grip and a gunshot shattered the uneasy peace, making the dozing dogs down at the north end of town spring up and bark like crazy.

But the bullet went wide and dug a chunk of adobe out of the cantina wall, three feet away from the sergeant.

Jake's eyes bugged. The sergeant was still dragging out his pistol. Recklessly

Jake fired again, and this time the sergeant opened his mouth and cried out. He dropped his pistol, grabbed for his left arm, from which a streamer of blood had erupted, and then corkscrewed to the sand, wailing like a widow.

The corporal stood frozen as he watched his companion curl into a ball. Some of the swarthiness left his face, but his eyes tightened up a little with anger. Jake saw that he too was considering going for his gun, and Jake dearly did not want that to happen.

'Start scratchin' the clouds, corporal!' he snapped firmly. 'Lessen you want perforatin', too!'

The corporal was furious, but not so foolish as to disobey. He raised his hands slowly and said, '*Bastardo!*'

Jake ignored the insult, glanced anxiously up and down the street and asked instead, 'Any more o' you boys around here?'

'Si. Twelve, fifteen.'

'I don't see 'em.'

'They're here.'

It was Jake's turn to reach a decision.

'You know what, corporal? I think you're bluffin'. I think you two were here alone. Am I right?'

The corporal said, 'Go to hell!'

Jake extended his gun-arm so that the Peacemaker's barrel was no more than a foot away from the corporal's face. 'Am I *right?*' he asked again.

It hurt him to admit it, but a couple of pulse-beats later the corporal said, 'Yes, you're right. But you won't — '

'Shut up,' Jake said. He moved around behind the *federale* and quickly relieved him of his handgun. Shoving the weapon into his own belt, he said, 'Go over to the well an' finish fillin' those skins for me. Quickly now, or you'll never live to see another sunset.'

He threw a quick glance down at the wounded sergeant, who was still curled up and nursing his shattered arm. Around them the road was still empty. Even the dogs had stopped their howling.

The corporal did as he was told, but slowly. He was being humiliated, and he was trying hard to retain at least some of his dignity. 'So I was right, then?' he said as he capped the second skin. 'You *are* a gun-runner?'

'No,' Jake lied. 'I'm just a man who can't spare the time to argue with a bunch of Mexican soldiers, that's all.'

'You'll never get away with this, you know.'

'To hell with that. Jus' fill the goddam skins.'

At last he spied a few faces watching him from windows and half-open doors, but that was all. No-one came out to help or hinder him. Like as not, the people of Linosa just wanted him out of their town, him and the *federales* both.

'There,' the corporal said, having completed his task. He turned away from the well and said sincerely, 'I hope this water chokes you.'

Jake's mind was racing. He couldn't shake the feeling that he'd just painted himself into a corner. He jabbed the gun vaguely toward the corporal's navel and said, 'Take them skins over to the corral. You're gonna help me saddle up an' get the hell out of here.'

'Never — '

'You'll do it or I'll shoot you,' Jake said gravely. 'My saddle's the first one you'll come to. It's a California with a patched-up right-side fender.'

They went over to the corral together, Jake staying a little way behind the *federale* and almost strangling the butt of his .45.

As he eyed the horses in the public corral, a new thought occurred to him. The blood-bay was done in. An eighteen-mile trot through the night and a ten-mile canter through the early morning warmth had taken just about everything out of him. Besides which, the horse had probably gorged itself on grass in the last twenty minutes, and grown loggy from the water in the trough.

It was no mount upon which to make a getaway, then: not if its rider was serious about making his escape.

Jake spotted a fine, clean-limbed dun with three white stockings over at the far side of the corral. It stood at least seventeen hands at the shoulder, and had the sleek, grain-fed look of an Army mount. A *federale* mount.

'Saddle up that dun,' he ordered on the spur of the moment.

The corporal spun around, fury contorting his features. Jake had guessed right, then: it was the corporal's horse.

'Do it,' he said, thumbing back the Peacemaker's hammer. 'An' do it right corporal, 'cause I'll be watchin' real close — an' I know all the tricks.'

The corporal had no choice. He knew it, but he was having difficulty accepting it. He whistled to the dun and it came over at an easy walk, and while Jake watched, the corporal saddled up for him, then tied the water skins around the saddle-horn and led the animal out through the double gate and into the roadway.

'I will see that you die for this,' he spat, meeting Jake's eyes.

Jake didn't bother to reply. He simply closed the distance as fast as he could and used the Peacemaker to club the *federale* down. The corporal grunted. His chocolate-brown sombrero spilled away into the sand. He fell to his knees but went no further than that, so Jake hit him again, twice, and after that the corporal sprawled out in the sun, blood on his forehead but still breathing, at least.

Jake drew in a sharp, shuddery breath. His legs went rubbery beneath him. He wasn't used to all this chicanery. He threw another look at the sergeant over by the cantina. He'd thrown up, but now he was on his knees, watching Jake.

Jake didn't say a word. He just pulled himself up across the dun's broad back and wheeled the animal around to the south, and quit Linosa at a flat-out, back-snapping gallop.

He rode hard and fast, even though he knew deep down that it would be hours yet before any kind of pursuit party could be dispatched. He'd seen no telegraph wires leading to or from Linosa, and neither of the *federales* would be in any fit state to travel for a while. Besides which, the soldiers would almost certainly have to return to their barracks, wherever in hell that was, to make a full report before further action could be taken.

Still, that didn't stop Jake from getting as much speed out of the corporal's horse as he could, aches or no aches. Anxious to put distance between himself and the soldiers, he kept the animal going south, then southeast, away from the main trail, finally swinging a wide loop across the increasingly barren, arroyo-slashed plain to head back to the high ground where he'd left his partner.

He was only a quarter of a mile from the timber-topped rise when he spotted Harry's piebald in plain view at the bottom of the slope, picking at some scrubby brush.

At once he knew that something was wrong. Harry might be a greenhorn, but he wasn't so stupid as to let his mount go wandering off all by itself.

Jake slowed the dun to a trot and approached the other horse with caution. The animal had been off-saddled and rubbed down, but the bit was still between its big, yellow teeth. Fortunately, the trailing reins had stopped it from straying too far.

Jake reined in and squinted up the rise to the trees. Disquiet stirred sluggishly in his belly. Where was Harry? Why had he allowed his mount to wander off unchecked?

There was only one way to find out.

He slipped the Peacemaker from its holster and swallowed loudly. Although he'd been about nineteen hours without sleep now, he felt edgy and alert. He reached down, grabbed the piebald's reins and heeled the dun into a quick but careful ascent toward the timber.

They topped out without being challenged, and because Jake had no wish to skyline himself against the blinding sunlight any longer than he had to, he kept them going straight into the trees. The timber was gloomy. Sunlight spilling down through the sparse canopy of leaves above painted everything dusty green. For a moment Jake wanted to call out Harry's name, but knew better than to break the silence.

He went on for about thirty yards and then reined in again, peering ahead. The cottonwoods gave him only an indistinct, slatted view of the terrain. No birds sang, nothing stirred.

He felt that something was very badly

wrong now. Just before he'd left for Linosa, he'd told Harry to keep his eyes peeled, and if there was one thing in the kid's favour, it was his ability to follow orders. So where was he now? If anything had happened to him —

Suddenly struck by a terrible sense of foreboding, Jake heeled the dun back into motion and they wound deeper towards the centre of the arbour with the piebald following dutifully behind. After what seemed like forever, the trees thinned out, and when they finally reached the edge of the clearing, Jake reined in again.

The first thing he noticed was that the mules were nowhere in sight. The second thing was Harry, sprawled on his belly, as still as a statue.

The sight of his companion in such a state made Jake throw caution to the wind. Hell, if whoever had attacked the limey was still around, the sonofabitch'd had ample opportunity to bushwhack him before this, anyway.

He came down out of the saddle like a man half his age, quickly tethered the two horses to a nearby deadfall and blundered straight into the clearing, virtually falling to his knees beside his comrade.

'Harry?'

The Englishman made no movement whatsoever.

Jake turned him over. Harry's face was a mask of blood. The sight of it made the breath catch in Jake's throat. All at once the edgy alertness left him and he felt tired again: tired of running and hiding and everything else they'd had to do to bring Elliott Blaze's damned guns this far.

He called the Englishman's name again and shook him a little. Harry still didn't stir. Bewildered, Jake looked for the rise and fall of the younger man's chest, but didn't find it.

A tingle washed over his face as he realised that Harry was dead. He sagged a little. His head dipped forward and he gave a small, painful groan. Someone had stolen the guns, and killed Harry to get at them. But the guns were no longer important. Jake just wanted the sonsof-bitches who'd done for Harry.

He saw something from the corner of

his eye and reached over the body to pick up the Englishman's battered straw hat. He turned it gently in his hands. If it hadn't been for him, Harry would never have come on this trip. If it hadn't been for him, the kid would still be alive.

Jake knew he would carry the guilt of that with him for the rest of his days.

He looked down at the corpse and put a hand on its shoulder. 'I'll get 'em for you, kid,' he promised quietly. 'So help me, I'll get 'em.'

And the corpse said, 'Oooo . . . '

Jake pulled his hands back quickly. 'Eh?'

Behind their closed lids, Harry's eyes began to move. His mouth fell open and he drew in a deep, whistling breath. If it hadn't been for all the blood daubed on his face, he might only have been waking up from an afternoon nap.

'Harry?' Jake shook the Englishman again, almost afraid to build his hopes up. 'Harry! Is it you I'm talkin' to, or a spirit?'

Harry opened his eyes. They were bloodshot and glazed, but slowly, with effort, they began to focus.

The Englishman's voice was a weak, dry croak. 'I . . . what . . . ?'

Jake said, 'Hold on, kid. I'll fetch some water.'

Hurriedly he went to get one of the skins. When he brought it back, Harry was struggling to rise into a sitting position, one hand on the ground, the other on his forehead.

'Bloody hell,' he muttered. 'Somebody must have . . . clobbered me awfully . . . hard. I've got a bump the size of a cricket ball on my noggin . . .'

Jake's sense of relief chased away some of his fatigue. 'Jus' take it steady for a minute,' he advised, cradling the limey's head and holding the water skin to his cracked lips.

The water must have triggered Harry's memory, because as soon as he'd had his fill, his punished face took on a look of urgency and he struggled to stand up.

'The guns, Jake! The rotters took our guns!'

'All right, all right. No need to set your bowels aboilin'. Settle down . . . that's it

. . . Now: *who* took our guns?'

As Harry replied, Jake doused a kerchief in water and began to wipe some of the sticky, crusted blood off his face.

'I'm not sure . . . they took me by surprise. I suppose they saw you leave and decided that they'd never get a better chance.' He winced. 'They must've struck about half an hour after you left. Yes, that would be about right. They came from the north, I think . . . one of them just rushed at me and walloped me with a rifle-stock . . . I tried to get up but he hit me again.'

'How many were there?'

'I'm not sure. Six?'

'Mexicans? Bandits, like them other fellers we saw, the ones that did for them *rurales?*'

Harry went to shake his head, then thought better of it. 'No. The blighter who hit me was American, and so were his companions, as far as I could see.'

Jake pondered that, wondering what, if anything, it could possibly mean. As he'd already noted, *gringos* were uncommon south of the border. Could it be that this group had been following them ever since El Paso?

Harry had said they'd come up from the north, and a couple of nights ago he'd thought he heard someone on their back-trail. Somehow the whole sorry business had fallen apart.

Jake might have known it: things had been running too well. But what were they to do *now?* Neither of them was especially skilled with firearms. What could they hope to do when — *if* — they caught up with the gang of rattlers who'd made off with the weapons?

As Jake hunkered there beside his pale-faced partner, he thought about the run-in he'd had with the *federales* back in Linosa. It would be foolish to stay in Mexico any longer than they had to. But something told him that Elliott Blaze wouldn't take it kindly if they decided to head back north without making at least some attempt to retrieve the stolen weapons.

He rubbed at his sore eyes. He was too damn' beat to think straight right now. But suddenly he had it: or thought he did. They were forty-odd miles from the border, and twenty some miles from Los Caballos Mestenos. Looking at it that way, it made more sense to go on to their eventual destination than turn back. Once they reached Los Caballos Mestenos, they could explain what had happened to whoever was waiting there to meet them. That way they'd not only be doing something to square things for Elliott, they might also be able to encourage Villa's men to do something about retrieving the guns for themselves.

He put the notion to Harry and Harry agreed that it made more sense than simply cutting their losses and going on home. Then the young Englishman noticed the dun horse tethered to the deadfall and Jake told him all about the trouble he'd had in Linosa.

For a while after that they allowed themselves to relax. It was a little after one o'clock in the afternoon and nothing would be moving out there beyond the tree-shade until the sun started sinking westward and the land cooled off.

It had been a heck of a day. Eventually

Jake's eyes closed and he fell asleep for a couple of hours. Harry also tried to rest up, but he was too fidgety. Instead, he sat back against his up-ended Visalia saddle and bathed the lump on his forehead with cool water to help the swelling go down.

When Jake woke up in the late afternoon and asked him if he felt well enough to ride, Harry said sure. He didn't look all that steady on his legs, though, so Jake saddled up the piebald for him. Each of them felt hungry now, but since their supplies had been filched along with the guns, they had to make do with a swallow or two of water.

Still, there was one thing to be said for having the mules and weapons stolen: their speed, as they crossed the arid flatlands, increased dramatically.

Soon the terrain began to dip and rise in a series of gentle, mesquite-speckled swells. Weathered rocks the colour of milky coffee soared skyward in all kinds of peculiar shapes to either side of the trail. A Chuckawalla, sunning his long, reptilian body on one oval boulder, watched the two men journey on south, riding slump-shouldered and with one eye constantly on their back-trail.

As usual, the travelling grew easier after dark. Jake felt less anxious with every mile he put between himself and Linosa. Harry rode beside him, silent and swaying. The egg-sized lump on his forehead throbbed with enough force to make him heave dryly. Jake glanced at him from time to time, just to make sure he was okay, and each time Harry forced a smile and nodded to say that he was.

Sometime after midnight, though, he passed out, and it was only by luck that Jake was able to reach across and steady him before he could tumble from the saddle.

They rested up for a while in the shadows of a wide, sandy crater. Jake spilled some water over Harry's sweat-run face, then forced some more down his throat. Around them the moon-washed land stretched away bone-white through the gloom.

'I'm sorry, Jake . . . wasting time like this . . . ' the Englishman panted weakly.

'Forget it,' Jake replied. 'I'm feelin' kind

of woozy myself. It's hunger that's doin' it.'

'Yes . . . probably.' Harry forced a grim chuckle. 'Oh for a steak and kidney pie, eh?'

'Or some ham an' eggs.'

'Or cod and chips.'

'Or a bowl of red-hot chili.'

Both of them laughed tiredly. While Harry sat quietly, getting some of his strength back, Jake checked on the horses. Fortunately the animals were both in sound condition, and only marginally winded by the distance they'd already covered tonight.

After a time, Jake asked Harry how he felt. Harry understood perfectly the question behind the question, and replied, 'Well enough to ride on.'

Even so, Jake held their pace down. Speed was not as important now as just maintaining a steady, mile-eating canter that was easier on the limey.

Within an hour or two, the land flattened out again, then gave way to a wide, rocky slope across which grew spiky Joshua trees and the odd palo verde.

Somewhere along the way they'd lost all track of distance. They knew they'd been riding for an awful long time, and that dawn couldn't be far away, but when Jake tried to estimate that distance in miles, he was stuck. It could have been ten, it could have been twenty or thirty. He just wasn't sure —

'*Alto!*'

The voice came down through the pre-dawn air from out of a long jumble of rocks about ten yards to the east. It was a strong, deep voice full of authority, and there was something about it that said it had better be obeyed, or else.

Recognising that, Jake hauled back on his reins straight away, and Harry followed his lead.

'*Conforme! Esta bien!*' Jake yelled to the darkness. Then; 'Quickly, kid — stick your hands up.'

Only then, when the surprise of it had worn off and it became apparent that they weren't going to be shot down in cold blood, did a mixture of anger and frustration well up inside Jake. To get caught after coming this far! Was there no end to his bad luck?

'No sudden moves, either of you!' snapped the Mexican up in the rocks. 'There are five guns covering you, so don't try anything foolish!'

Harry glanced across at Jake, a question on his face. Jake shook his head slightly and whispered, 'Do like he says.'

The voice might have been bluffing, but if it wasn't, they'd find out the hard way. A small, disturbed rock rolled down the shale slope. Both *gringos* turned their heads to look that way. They just about discerned three men descending the slope towards them. Two of them carried carbines, the third a stubby-looking shotgun.

Jake frowned. He'd been expecting to see *federale* uniforms, but these men were dressed in range-clothes. They weren't *vaqueros*, though: they were too heavily-armed for that. Bandits, then? Given the way they were behaving, that was a reasonable assumption. They were either bandits, he thought, or guards, keeping watch on the trail to Los Caballos Mestenos.

One of the Mexicans came forward while the other two kept the *gringos* covered. In the slowly-building light, Jake and Harry saw a short, stout fellow with thick Latin features and dark, glittering eyes. A bandolier stuffed with shells for the cut-down Purdey shotgun in his hands was draped across his barrel chest. He had a thick black moustache under his hooked nose, and stubble shading his weak chin.

'You are Villa's men?' Jake asked in Spanish.

The Mexican ignored the question, saying instead, '*Apearse.*'

'We had business here with Villa,' Jake tried again. 'That was — '

'*Apearse,*' repeated the stout Mexican.

'But — '

'Step down! Quickly now, an' no more arguments!'

Harry said mildly, 'Best do as he says, old chap. The last thing we want to do right now is upset the natives.'

They dismounted slowly and the other two Mexicans came down out of the rocks to join their companions on the greying trail. They all looked as hard as steel and suspicious of Anglos travelling through the night. The stout Mexican checked Harry over for weapons and confiscated the Colt 1911 A1, then relieved Jake of his .45 and the *federale* corporal's French pistol, which was still shoved behind his shell-belt.

The two failed gun-runners were shoved roughly over to the side of the trail and told to keep their hands up. For a moment there was only an uneasy trading of stares between the captives and their captors. Then a tallish Mexican pushed through the line of men to confront them head-on, a slim, elegantly-attired fellow with a long, pock-marked face and the lean hips of a born horseman. He was about as old as Harry, mid-twenties, but his shrewd hazel eyes hinted at much greater experience: of men, of women, of living and of death.

The tall Mexican took the French pistol from his stout companion and held it in his palm, as if he were trying to judge its weight. At last he turned the gun around so that it was pointed at Jake's whiskery face. He said, 'You carry a *federale* weapon, *señor*. How can this be?'

Because he thought it might help his cause, Jake told the truth. 'I took it off a corporal who was after arrestin' me this mornin'.'

The tall Mexican clearly did not believe him. 'Oh?' His tone was mocking. 'And why did he want to arrest you? You are an outlaw, perhaps? A famous *Yanqui* badman?'

A couple of his comrades chuckled in appreciation of his sarcasm.

'No,' Jake replied, trying to keep his anger in check. 'Because he thought I was runnin' guns down here to Pancho Villa.'

Some of the humour vanished from the Mexicans' faces. Jake new he'd struck some kind of a nerve in them, and he pressed his advantage. 'Look, you're Villa's men, *si*? You are *revolucionarios*, yes?' He got no reply, but that didn't matter: he just kept going. 'My friend and I, we were bringing guns to Villa, to a place called Los Caballos Mestenos.'

The tall Mexican who'd been doing all the interrogating stiffened. 'Where did you get that information?' he demanded.

158

'From a feller named Elliott Blaze,' Jake replied, still using Spanish. 'We were to deliver the guns to Los Caballos Mestenos no later than tomorrow . . . well, today as it is now. We weren't given any names, jus' told that one of Villa's agents would be expectin' us.'

The Mexican was still leery of them. 'I don't see any guns *with* you,' he said after a moment. 'All I see are two sorry-lookin' *gringos*, trying to lie their way out of a quick death.'

'The guns were stolen,' Jake told them tightly. 'Early this mornin'. While I was havin' that little set-to with them *federales* I jus' told you about, they cold-cocked my partner here an' made off with the merchandise.'

'You're lyin',' the Mexican said again.

Harry stepped forward and pointed to the ugly, purplish lump on his forehead. 'Take a look at this if you don't believe us,' he invited indignantly. 'That's where one of them cracked me with his rifle-stock.'

Jake took some comfort from the low muttering that went through the rest of them. He thought they might be starting to believe him at last.

The tallish Mexican squinted at Harry. Behind him, the sun was just starting to fire up a new day. 'These men you say stole the guns away from you,' he said. 'Could you describe them?'

Harry shook his head. 'No. It all happened too fast. But they were Americans, as near as I could tell. Not Mexicans.'

Jake watched the tall man for a reaction. He wasn't disappointed. It wasn't much of a response, but there was a definite tightening of the muscles around the fellow's eyes and mouth when he heard what Harry had to say.

All of a sudden the tall man reached a decision. Turning to his stout *compadre* he said, 'Pablo, you and Jesus fetch our horses.' To Jake and Harry he added, 'To be honest with you, I'm not sure *what* to believe. That's why I'm takin' you in, so that *el jefe* himself can question you. If you're tellin' the truth, you will be unharmed. But if you are lyin' . . . well, you dig your own graves before we kill you, my friends.'

7

Los Caballos Mestenos was not a town, as Jake had expected, it was a horse-ranch: and a rather prosperous-looking one at that.

Surprisingly fertile pasture-land shelved away to the south, west and east of the main yard, which was comprised mainly of hard-packed dirt. A big adobe house of typical Spanish design dominated the yard, white-walled and red-tiled, all arches and pillars.

Away to the south stood a low bunkhouse, also of adobe, and across from that rose a plank-built livery barn and stable, behind which several fine horses grazed and frolicked in a spacious, high-walled corral.

The place was very much a working concern, Jake saw as he and Harry were herded down an easy slope and on towards the yard. A well-kept wagon stood off to one side of the bunkhouse, and the hot, spicy aromas of Mexican food wafted from the nearby cookhouse, making the prisoners' guts rumble violently.

Some of the *vaqueros* going about their duties down in the yard stopped what they were doing to watch the newcomers' approach. Jake noticed that all of them carried a sidearm of some description, many of them more than one.

At last the tallish Mexican brought his little party to a halt outside the main house and dismounted gracefully, leaving his beautiful bay horse ground-hitched. Without a word he left the rest of them sitting in their saddles beneath a strengthening sun, went up onto the porch and straight inside through the wide door.

Harry was wilting a little. Leaning across to him, Jake said, 'You feelin' all right, kid?'

'*No talkin' there!*' snapped the stout Mexican, whose name was Pablo.

Jake threw a venomous look over his shoulder. 'I'm askin' him how he feels,' he barked with scant regard for the consequences, 'not tellin' him to make a break for it!'

When Jake turned back to his partner, he found Harry's eyes on him. 'I'm fine,' the Englishman said with a game smile.

The tallish Mexican came back out of the house and stabbed one long finger at the prisoners. *'Apearse! Vamos!'* They dismounted. The tallish Mexican said, 'Inside, now. Turn left inside the hallway and go through the door at the far end. And no tricks. I'll be coverin' you all the way.'

To prove it, he took Harry's automatic from his waistband and indicated that they should go ahead of him. The house was cool, and the walls, which were three feet thick, and the jugs, or *ollas*, filled with water and hung at strategic points to keep the air moist, would ensure that it stayed that way all day, no matter how hot it grew outside. There wasn't a single speck of dust in the place, and the furnishings spoke of wealth and comfort.

The room at the far end of the hallway was a dining room, long, wide and, like the rest of the place, low-ceilinged. Sunshine poured in through a long, curtainless window, bouncing off the

163

plain white walls in a clean, pleasant spill.

A mahogany table sat in the centre of the room, long enough to seat twelve guests comfortably. But the room's only occupant was a man who was standing at the head of the table, just in front of a huge fireplace. Over the fireplace were the room's only two objects of decoration: a large silver crucifix and a framed chromolithograph of the Virgin.

The man standing at the head of the table had his hands folded behind his back. He watched the tall Mexican herd Jake and Harry into the room, then gestured that they should be seated.

They did as they were told. Only then did they become aware of other sounds going on in the house: the high, relaxed laughter of a couple of young girls, perhaps servants making beds, and the sizzlings and clatterings that Jake always associated with a busy kitchen.

His empty belly fairly churned at the thought of food. But there were more pressing concerns to occupy him now. He returned the appraisal of the man over by the cold fireplace, *el jefe*, the headman, as their tall, pock-faced captor had called him.

El jefe was short and pudgy, with a round, fleshy face, piercingly dark eyes and a heavy black moustache curving like a down-turned horseshoe beneath his Roman nose. He was dressed in a pair of rumpled grey California pants, a white shirt and a short black jacket with fancy gold needlework at the cuffs and collar. He looked tired but authoritative.

'So,' he said in Spanish. 'You are the *gringos* Felix here told me about. The *gringos* who were to deliver some guns to me.'

Jake squinted up at the man. 'You are Villa's agent?' he asked, also in Spanish.

El jefe smiled. 'I am *Villa*,' he said simply.

Jake's surprise showed on his face. Never in a month of Sundays had he thought to come face to face with the bandit revolutionary himself.

Pancho Villa said, 'This business puzzles me.'

'Why? It's plain enough what happened. Elliott Blaze hired us to deliver some guns and ammunition. The merchandise was stolen. We could have turned tail an' gone straight back home. Instead we came here to tell you what had happened.' Jake shrugged wearily. 'We've got nothin' to gain by lying' to you, *Señor* Villa.'

'I know,' Villa returned. 'But still I am puzzled.'

Again Jake said, '*Por que?* Why?'

'Because the guns were delivered here yesterday afternoon.'

'What?'

'Exactly.'

Villa waited a moment, then turned his intense black eyes onto the tall Mexican, Felix. 'Fetch coffee for these men,' he said. Felix left the room. They all listened to the sound his footsteps made on the hallway floor.

At last Harry said, 'Jake — what's going on? All I've heard so far is a lot of foreign chatter.'

Briefly, Jake translated the gist of the conversation for the Englishman's benefit, then turned back to Villa, who was watching them. 'Is it possible that your deal with Blaze could've leaked out?'

'No. The details of this transaction — as with all the business I conduct with *Señor* Blaze — are known only to a few trusted aides.'

'But somebody knew enough about it to rob us and sell the guns on to you, here.' Jake paused. 'Ah, no offense, general, but . . . how much did you pay for them?'

'Eight thousand American dollars.'

Jake frowned. 'I thought the price you agreed with Elliott was ten thousand.'

'It was,' said Villa. 'But according to the men who delivered the weapons yesterday, *Señor* Blaze could not supply part of the order.'

'Which part?'

'The twelve Lewis guns.'

Harry, who didn't understand a word of Spanish, said, 'Will somebody please tell me what's going on?'

Jake ignored him. He kept his eyes on Villa as he said, 'We fetched those Lewis guns forty miles from the Rio before whoever robbed us got hold of 'em, tripods an' all. I should know: I checked an' packed everythin' away myself the night we left El Paso.'

Villa's brows met beneath a corrugated forehead. 'This affair grows more curious by the minute,' he said pensively.

Jake was inclined to agree. 'You did business with these men, general. How many of them were there?'

'Four.'

'My buddy here says he thinks there were six of 'em when they jumped him. All *Yanquis*.'

'Perhaps the other two took the Lewis guns on ahead to another customer.'

'That's what I'm thinkin'. Does anyone spring to mind?'

Villa shrugged. 'Not immediately. Emiliano Zapata. Venustiano Carranza. But I doubt it. These weapons *Señor* Blaze supplied, they were intended for the good of us all. Besides, the Lewis guns were expensive. Two thousand dollars to me, as an old and valued customer. Worth considerably more than that on the open market.'

'So we're lookin' for a customer with plenty of money at his disposal.'

Villa turned his round face towards the sunlight. He had a certain hardness about him, despite his bulk, and Jake found it easy to picture him as a bandit. Seeing him as a champion of the people, however, took considerably more effort.

'You've got someone in mind?' he prompted.

Villa nodded. '*Si*, though I pray to God that I am wrong. The *federales, señor*. General Huerta's army.'

'Huh? But I thought — '

Felix came back into the room carrying a tray. As he set it down and poured coffee for them all, the bandit general said, 'You thought that the arms embargo your President Wilson imposed this past summer forbade the supply of all weapons to Mexico except those intended for use by the Mexican army, *si?*'

'Well . . . yeah.'

'This is correct.'

'Then why would Huerta need to buy weapons from gun-runners?'

'Because the supply of arms from your country is slow and unreliable, and made slower by the *roja cinta*, what you would call governmental red tape. If Huerta could obtain weapons — especially Lewis guns — any faster from other sources, he would do so willingly, my friend.'

Felix, who had been listening to all of this, suddenly swore. '*Perdon, jefe,* but . . . is this true? That the men who delivered those guns to us yesterday are also supplying the *federales?*'

'It is possible,' Villa admitted. He gave the matter some more thought, then said, 'Felix: you are to accord these men every courtesy. See that they have food and rest, and anything else they need.'

'*Si, jefe.*'

'Send out your best trackers, too. At once. I want to know which way those gun-runners went when they left here last evening.'

Felix clicked his heels smartly. 'It will be done, general.'

At last Villa turned his eyes back onto Jake and Harry, who were savouring the thick black coffee. 'I am grateful to you for your honesty,' he said formally. 'I have found that it is a rare trait where Anglos are concerned. But your friend there,

Señor Tanner, the hombre with the funny straw hat, he was wrong. There was at least one Mexican with the men who delivered the guns. It was with him that I conducted our business.'

Something dark and suspicious shifted around at the back of Jake's mind. 'Who was he, this Mexican? What did he look like?'

Villa thought. 'Tall, thin, about thirty years of age.'

'Did he have a moustache? A thin one?'

Villa's gaze sharpened. '*Si*. You know him?'

'A little,' Jake replied grimly. 'Lessen I'm mistaken, that was Miguel — Elliott Blaze's goddam manservant.'

★ ★ ★

That revelation answered some of it, but by no means all.

With a troubled frown, Villa excused himself and left them alone. It became Jake's turn to stare pensively through the window. At last Harry could stand the suspense no longer. Although he was lousy with languages, he was pretty sharp on tones, and he knew that something important was going on.

'Come on, Jake — out with it, old boy.'

Jake blinked a couple of times, coming out of his reverie, then gave the Englishman a potted recap on everything that he and Villa had spoken about.

At the end of it, Harry clenched his fists angrily. 'Well, bugger behold!' he breathed, pointing to the lump on his head. 'So I have Elliott Blaze to thank for this, do I?'

Jake shook his head. 'No — you got *Miguel* to thank for it.'

'But Miguel works for Elliott.'

'*Worked.* Lessen I miss my guess, he's playin' a lone hand now.'

'Why do you say that?'

'Because the guns were Elliott's property,' Jake replied simply. 'He could've sold 'em to whoever he liked without any o' this funny business.' His brown eyes took on a faraway glaze as he brought order to his thoughts. 'No — it's my feelin' that Miguel planned this all by hisself. He let Elliott hire a couple of good men to take all the risks gettin' the guns across the Rio, then stole 'em away when he judged the time was right.'

'The sneaky sod,' said Harry.

There was a noise over at the dining room door. Pablo, the stout Mexican with the bandolier draped across his barrel chest, cleared his throat and said, 'There is food over at the cookhouse, *señores:* enough hot water for a couple good baths, too.'

That news perked Jake up a bit. 'Well, we c'd sure use a little spruce-up,' he allowed, rising. 'Come on, kid. We're the guests of Pancho Villa hisself now. Might as well enjoy the experience.'

Harry's mouth cracked into a smile. 'Ra-*ther!*'

Pablo led them back outside and across the yard. Jake asked him where their horses were and Pablo told him they had been taken away to the stable.

In the cookhouse a miserly little Mexican with white hair and a neck like that of a buzzard urged them to sit at a long trestle table and then set heaped platters of bacon and beans before them.

173

The food worked wonders. It chased away Jake's fatigue and helped to clear Harry's persistent headache.

As good as the food undoubtedly was, however, the baths they took out behind the bunkhouse worked an even more beneficial effect. After a lengthy soak and a shave, the Anglos climbed back into their dusty clothes and headed into the bunkhouse, where they chose a couple of bunks near the door and stretched out to enjoy their first really decent sleep in days. Neither man dreamed. Maybe they were too exhausted to dream. Whatever, they slept on, undisturbed, until a sudden pounding of boots on floorboards woke them up.

At first Jake didn't know where he was. Oh, bunkhouse surroundings were familiar enough. But who in hell were all these damn' chili-eaters storming through the doorway and grabbing rifles from a rack on the wall?

It was the rifles that explained everything. Rifles. Guns. This whole business had been about guns.

Just across the aisle from him, Harry

was sitting up and watching all the activity, clearly as perplexed as his partner.

At last the tallish Mexican, Felix, hurried in, pocked face set in grim lines. It was the middle of the afternoon, if the position of the shadows outside were anything to go by.

Jake got his feet under him, stood up and asked, '*Que pasa?*'

He had to tap Felix on the forearm and ask the question again before the tall revolutionary answered him.

'What did he say, Jake?' Harry asked after Felix finished speaking and went over to the rifle rack to hurry his men along.

Jake rubbed his jaw. 'Says they found the tracks Miguel's boys left behind 'em las' night. The way they read it, the four buckos who did the deal with Villa met their two buddies about three miles to the south an' east.'

'The other two had the Lewis guns with them,' Harry guessed.

Jake nodded. 'That's how it looks.'

'So Villa's men are going after them?'

'They've got no option, by the sound of it. The way Felix there tells it, Miguel's bunch looks like it's headed for a scrubby little ghost town 'bout thirty, forty miles southeast. By all accounts, there were some *federale* troop movements down that way a couple weeks back.'

'So Villa might be right,' Harry said urgently. 'Miguel could be planning to sell those Lewis guns to the *federales*.'

Now armed to the teeth, the *vaqueros* began to head for the door. As he passed them, Pablo paused just long enough to toss Jake's Peacemaker and Harry's automatic onto Harry's rumpled bunk. The two Anglos frowned down at their side-arms, not quite sure how they should read the gesture.

Felix must have been watching them and seen their indecision, because he too paused before quitting the bunkhouse and said, 'Your horses are waiting outside. You may ride north, back to your own country, or you may ride with us, to glory.'

He didn't wait for a reply, just brushed past them and went to join his men in mounting up.

Jake and Harry exchanged a loaded glance. The temptation to cut their losses and leave the revolution to the Mexicans was awful strong. But each of them knew that until they got hold of Elliott's money, they could hardly go return home. Villa might somehow find a way of sending it on, but then again, he might not.

Like it or not, then, they had no choice: they had to be in at the kill.

The heat slapped them in the face as they hustled outside. It was a hell of a time to go riding, probably the worst. As they hurried along to the hitch-rack where their mounts had been tethered, Villa came across the yard on his stubby, bowed legs, round face grim and flushed, intense eyes bright beneath the shade of his sombrero.

He rattled out some instructions in Spanish, and when he was through Harry leaned over to his partner and whispered, 'What was all that about?'

Jake was obviously puzzled. 'Not sure. Near as I can work it, he was warnin' us to look out for a place in Rhode Island.'

'Eh?'

Jake shrugged. 'That's what he said. 'Remember: watch out for the 'Newport''.'

Harry thought about it, then said, 'He must have said 'Nieuport'.'

'There's a difference?'

'A Nieuport is a biplane.'

Jake's shoulders slumped despondently. 'Aw, don't tell me the *federales* got one o' them things flappin' around these parts as well.'

'Looks that way.'

Felix saluted his general, then wheeled his bay horse around and galloped out of the yard, headed southeast. His men, who numbered ten, followed him in a strung-out, hard-riding line.

Jake and Harry kept roughly in the middle of the column. Felix led them up over the rolling pastureland. Jake spotted more men out in the lush fields, working with horses or cattle or the land itself. Then the ranch fell behind them and they were out in open country.

'We estimate that this Miguel and his *compadres* are perhaps twenty five or thirty miles ahead,' said Pablo, spurring his calico mare up alongside them. He spoke surprisingly good English, so that Harry would understand him.

The Englishman gave a low whistle. 'My goodness! Do you think we can possibly catch up with them?'

'We had better,' Pablo replied gravely. 'But then why should we not? We are riding fast. They will be taking their time, unaware that we are after them.'

That was true, Jake supposed. That he and Harry had continued on to Los Caballos Mestenos instead of turning back was the last thing Miguel would have expected: at least that's what they were all counting on.

The afternoon was scorching. Before the column had gone much more than a dozen miles, men and horses both were wilting. Felix sent scouts out ahead to pick up sign, and rested the remainder of his column at short but frequent intervals. Even so, the pursuit took its toll on them all, even after the sun went down and there was some respite from the torridity.

At length, when darkness came creeping in from the east, Felix called a halt for the day. They found a verdant bowl of land screened from the west by trees and the south by rocks, and Felix posted guards while the rest of the men saw to the comfort of their horses. All of them were bone-weary, and dealt with their various chores in the quiet, orderly way that tired men frequently do.

Once Harry had turned his piebald out into a roped-off patch of grama grass, he flopped down on the fringe of the camp, took off his straw hat and mopped at his bruised brow. Jake, standing some way off, watched him thoughtfully through gritty, sore eyes. The last few days had been tough on the kid, but he'd met the challenge of them manfully. But unless he was mistaken, Harry was now reaching the end of his reserves.

Jake shuffled over to him. When he was near enough he hunkered down and said, 'You all right, boy?'

Harry looked up and offered him a brief smile. 'Oh . . . yes.'

His voice was hollow, though, and Jake picked up on it right away. 'Somethin' on your mind?'

The Englishman paused before answering, uncertain how best to explain his problem. At last he said soberly, 'It's going to be rough, isn't it? When we catch up with Miguel, I mean. It's going to be bloody.'

Jake considered. 'That'll depend on one of two things,' he replied. 'Whether or not Felix gives him the chance to surrender: and whether or not Miguel's got sense enough to take it.'

It was his turn to pause a while. Then he said quietly, 'Listen . . . you don't have to be a part of this, Harry. You could light out right now, go on back to the ranch, an' not one man here would condemn you for it.'

'Oh, I couldn't do that, Jake. I've come this far: I've got to see it through to the end now.'

'Even if the end means seein' folks stoppin' bullets?'

Harry's smile was wan. 'Yes. Even then.'

About three hours later one of the guards gave a shout and the rest of the men, who'd been sleeping or playing cards or swapping gab, all came alert to the sounds of two horses, being ridden hard. Within minutes, the scouts Felix had sent out shortly after making camp slowed their heaving mounts and came trotting into the feeble orange glow of the single campfire, to be surrounded by their eager companions almost immediately.

Jake and Harry stood on the sidelines as Felix told the scouts to make their report. Once they were finished, Jake translated quietly. 'They cut sign about fifteen miles southeast. They reckon Miguel can't be much more'n two, three miles beyond that.'

Felix spoke some more rapid-fire Spanish and some of the other men bobbed their heads or muttered assent. Jake said, 'Looks like we'd better bed down early, boy. We're movin' out an hour before dawn. Felix wants to catch Miguel while the bastard's still got sleep in his eyes.'

The night passed quickly. Although Harry thought he might have trouble sleeping, he dropped off almost as soon as he closed his eyes. The next time he opened them, Jake and the Mexicans were saddling up in tense silence.

The young Englishman got to his feet and shivered at the pre-dawn chill. As he hustled across to the rope corral to prepare his own horse for riding, he felt the solid, deadly weight of the Colt automatic in his waistband, and wondered grimly if the time had finally come for him to use it to kill.

8

They rode grimly, in silence. Felix sent two more scouts ahead. Even before the first misleading grey streaks of false dawn could be seen in the still-dark sky, their camp lay several miles behind them.

The land was wrinkled now, for they were entering foothills prior to rising yet higher into a vast and desolate mountain range. The narrow trail was littered with rocks and fringed with stunted, half-dead trees. They made their steady ascent in single file. According to Pablo, the town to which they were convinced Miguel was heading was situated about ten miles straight ahead. Its remote high-country location had been one of the main reasons for its demise several years earlier. Now it was just a cluster of skeletal frame dwellings and tumble-down adobes, its only occupants rats, snakes and possibly a bunch of *javelinas*, or desert pigs.

'And who knows?' the stout Mexican

finished grimly. 'Maybe even *federales*, too.'

Felix's scouts came back within an hour. Felix called a halt to hear what they had to say. They had located Miguel's campsite, which was on high ground about two miles away. The former manservant's camp had been set up beside a malnourished trickle of water, and was protected on all sides by timber.

'He had the guns, this Miguel?' asked Felix.

One of the scouts dipped his head. '*Si, patron.* Six long crates, three mules.'

'Guards?'

The scout held two fingers. '*Dos.*'

Felix thought for a moment, then said '*Matar ellos.*'

Harry leaned across to Jake and hissed, 'What did he say?'

Jake replied without looking at him. 'He said to kill 'em.'

The two scouts showed no reaction to the order, neither pleasure nor reluctance. They simply wheeled their horses around and galloped back up the trail, eventually disappearing into the gloom.

185

Felix led the rest of them on at a trot. When they finally caught up with the scouts' tethered mounts, he used a few sharp hand-signals to tell the others to do likewise.

They waited for a while in the dawning light. It was still cold this early, and vapour wreathed their mouths and nostrils. After a while, the scouts came down through the timber to the east. One of them was still wiping the thick blade of a wicked Bowie knife before sliding it back into its sheath.

Felix's expression asked the question. One of the scouts said simply, 'They are dead.'

'And the others?'

The scout's teeth flashed white through the semi-darkness. 'Sleepin' like babies.'

'Good work.'

Felix turned to the others and began to issue orders in a low but urgent tone. He had no elaborate plan of action. His only intention was to surround the remainder of the gun-runners and call upon them to surrender. What happened after he did that was entirely up to them.

Like wraiths Jake, Harry and the Mexicans ghosted up through the timber. The ground was hard and the incline was steep. Twice Jake nearly slipped on the dew-slick grass, and had to pause that many times again to get his breath back.

Ten minutes passed with only the small, barely-discernible sounds of men moving quietly up to the summit of the slope. Then Harry, who was a little off to Jake's left, suddenly froze and gave a startled gasp, and when Jake looked his way he saw one of the guards sprawled on his back beside a tree, eyes wide and sightless, throat slit from ear to ear.

Miguel's camp couldn't be far above them now, then. As if by some mute agreement, they all went down low and snaked the rest of the way. Almost at once the timber gave way to knee-high brush and weeds, and just beyond that, where the high ground cleared altogether, they saw the camp.

Miguel's horses and mules had been picketed on the particularly lush grass beside a thin, shallow stream that cut the clearing in two. About thirty feet away,

Jake counted four blanket-draped figures around the blackened smudge of a dead campfire. Six long crates — part of the same shipment Jake and Harry had fetched forty-odd miles from the border — had been piled over by the northeast perimeter of the camp, beside a mess of saddles, bridles, bits and blankets.

The clearing was absolutely silent. Jake turned his head, panning his gaze from left to right across the timber on the far side of the stream. The men Felix had told to approach from that side sure knew their business: he spotted them only with effort.

Felix was watching for them too, waiting until they were all in position. The air was tense. The dawn sky was a bleak, funereal grey. Harry hardly dared to breathe for fear that the sleeping men would hear him and be forewarned.

At last Felix judged the time to be right. Rising up with a Mauser pistol in his fist, he burst through the brush and into the clearing, yelling, '*Despertarse, cabrones!* Wake up, you're surrounded!'

The rest of the Mexicans followed his

lead, so Jake and Harry did, too, and as the four sleeping men suddenly boiled up out of their blankets with their sleep-puffed eyes wide with surprise, Villa's men stormed into the open, armed to the teeth and ready to fight.

For a moment the clearing echoed to the confused shouts of the startled men. They didn't know for sure what was happening, only that something was desperately wrong.

One of them, perhaps more foolish than the rest or of quicker reactions, brought a Smith & Wesson up from beneath his blanket. He fired the gun twice before bullets from two Mexican rifles tossed him backwards and made mincemeat of his chest.

Another of them, perhaps still uncertain of the overwhelming odds he could never hope to buck, also tried to make a fight of it. Jake was standing about sixty feet away when the sonofabitch brought out a Greener shotgun he'd been using as a sleeping partner. There were three of Villa's men on that side of the clearing, Pablo and two others, and even as Jake yelled for them to watch out, he knew he was too late.

The shotgun boomed and the three Mexicans fell away like leaves in an autumn wind.

But retaliation was swift. More gunfire blasted across the clearing even before the roar of the shotgun had left the air, and lead did unspeakable things to the *Yanqui*'s head, chest and shoulder, chopping him up and twisting him around in a violent crimson shower.

Miguel and the remaining *gringo* both reached for the sky fast and started yelling that there was no need for anyone else to die, that they were surrendering, see? Jake doubted whether either of them knew for sure what was going on, but even half-asleep, a man knows that he doesn't want to hop the twig.

Felix barked a few sharp orders. Two of his men went over to Miguel and the *gringo*, roughly relieved them of their weapons and booted them in the ribs to get them to roll onto their bellies and lay flat.

Meanwhile, Jake joined Felix in hustling across the clearing to check on their fallen comrades. Harry was already there, kneeling beside the trio. He saw the two shadows fall onto the grass beside him and said shakily, 'Pablo's dead. These other two . . . they're wounded, this one — '

'Raul.'

' — quite seriously, by the look of things. The other one isn't so bad.'

Felix called for a tall, gangling fellow in a fancy *vaquero's* suit, whose name was Pino. Jake assumed that Pino knew something about medicine, because as soon as he came over, he knelt beside the wounded men and went to work trying to patch them up.

Harry got to his feet and moved back a step, to get out of the way. He looked paler than bleached flour. Jake noticed the still-smoking automatic in his fist and said, 'You use that thing, boy?'

Harry suddenly became aware of the Colt. He looked at it for a moment, then nodded. 'I . . . I suppose I did, yes.'

'You hit what you was aimin' at?'

191

Harry's sick eyes lingered on the bullet-riddled shotgun man stretched out twenty feet away. 'Your guess is as good as mine, old boy,' he replied, sticking the automatic back into his waistband.

There was nothing that Felix could do for the wounded men. Pino was handling that chore. So the pock-faced Mexican turned on his heel and went over to the two spread-eagled prisoners, and Jake and Harry followed him.

Miguel was dressed in dusty range wear. He didn't look half so prissy sprawled flat on his belly, craning his neck to look up at his captors. He looked scared, desperate and on the verge of tears. The American with him had more grit. He stared up at Felix through hard, defiant eyes. He looked as tough as steel and twice as cold.

Felix stared at them with his jaw muscles working overtime. Miguel was babbling something about this being a mistake. Then he recognised Jake, realised that this was not just one bunch of robbers preying on another, that it was all to do with the guns, and started jabbering for mercy instead.

Jake fixed him with a flinty glare. 'You know somethin' Miguel?' he said mildly. 'I'm kind of disappointed in you.'

Miguel just looked at him for a moment. Then he said that this whole episode had been just a foolish notion, a moment of greed, and then, halfway through, he suddenly changed tack. He started to say that the *gringos*, they were responsible for all of this, that they had forced him into taking part in their treachery —

The American stretched out beside him said, 'Why, you lyin' bastard!'

Felix addressed him in English. 'It was Miguel's idea, then, eh? To take the Lewis guns on to the *federales* instead of sellin' them to Villa with the rest of the shipment?'

The American spat. 'Damn' right.'

Jake chimed in. ''Nother straight answer, mister. Did Elliott Blaze have anythin' to do with this?'

The American frowned and said, 'Who's Elliott Blaze?'

That was answer enough for Jake. As

he'd thought all along, Elliott had obviously had nothing to do with it.

Turning his attention back to Miguel, he said tiredly, 'Where's the money?'

Miguel, knowing that he was well and truly sunk, just replied, '*Compassion, por favor . . .* '

'Mercy be damned!' Felix spat in disgust. He looked over at Harry. 'Check through his saddlebags. You'll find the cash there, I'll bet.'

Harry was halfway over to the mess of saddles and bridles when Pino called out, 'Raul jus' died, *patron.*'

Felix took the news without so much as a twitch of the mouth. His dark eyes were absolutely unreadable. He said to Jake, 'Have you any more questions?' and when Jake shook his head no, Felix calmly brought up his Mauser pistol and shot each of the prisoners through the top of the head.

Jake was as startled as the rest of the Mexicans. He couldn't help flinching as the 7.63mm bullets punched through hair and bone and Miguel and the American twitched once, then lay still.

Somehow he tore his eyes away from the fresh corpses and opened his mouth to say something, but before he could voice what he was feeling — mainly horror, revulsion and anger — Felix said simply, '*Esto es guerra, señor*. This is war.'

He turned to address the rest of them, his voice sharp and businesslike. 'All right, we've got the guns: now let's get away from here! If there *are* any *federales* in this region, all this gunfire will bring them runnin' before too much longer!'

Jake was still shaken, but he guessed that Felix had a point. Suddenly the clearing was a hive of activity. Some of the men prepared the three mules for travel, then set about loading the crates aboard the pack-trees. A couple more took their dead comrades by the arms and legs and carried them back down the slope to the tethered horses. While Jake and Harry watched, Miguel and the rest of his crew were systematically stripped of everything of value, then left where they were, food for wolves and worms.

Somehow Jake forced the memory of

the two executions from his mind. There were other things to occupy him now, things that didn't necessarily have to do with blood and gristle. 'You find the cash, boy? Harry?'

'Eh?'

'You . . . you find Elliott's money?'

Harry was also shaken by the double execution, but he'd quickly checked through the gathered saddlebags, and now produced an old tin box from one of them. 'I think so. This looks promising . . . '

He opened the box and a sizeable wad of American paper currency stared back up at them. 'Yes . . . this is it.'

Jake took it for safekeeping. 'Good. Now all we gotta do is get the other two thousand from Villa an' we can head for home,' he said quietly.

He just couldn't wait now, and he knew that Harry shared his eagerness to get back to the relative safety, and sanity, of American soil.

'You have what you want?'

They looked around. It was Felix. Jake nodded. 'Yeah.'

'Then let's move!'

They left the clearing at the double, went back down the timber-studded slope and quickly toed into leather. The bodies of Pablo and Raul had been tied across their horses, much to the horses' disquiet, and the wounded man was slumped in his saddle, looking ashen as his mouth worked loosely in silent prayer.

Felix inspected what was left of his band, then wheeled his bay horse around, pointed north and west. 'All right, *mi hermanos!*' he cried. 'Let's ride!'

The high, sharp report of a rifle-shot cracked through air just then, and Felix said, 'Unh!' and jerked violently and hunched forward with blood dribbling down the back of his shirt.

Harry's eyes widened as he stabbed a finger at something further along the trail, and yelled, '*Federales!*'

The cry threw Villa's men into confusion. Jake, grabbing for his Peacemaker, saw a whole bunch of government troops fighting to steady their own prancing mounts some forty yards up the trail, about fifteen of them at least. He brought the .45 up, knowing he was too far away to do any real good with a handgun, but at least the action stifled his natural impulse to panic.

Felix toppled from his bay horse and landed on some sharp rocks in the loose, careless way that dead men usually do. The *federales* fired down at the rest of Villa's men once more and the high country air quivered to the sound of the volley.

Bullets fell like rain. The wounded man cried out and slipped sideways off his nervy mount. Another of the Mexicans screamed and clutched at his shoulder. Jake fired another shot. Harry whipped out his automatic and followed suit.

Villa's men were still trying to control their surprised horses and launch some kind of concerted retaliation, but without a leader bawling commands at them, they might as well have been just another bunch of *peones*.

Maybe that was why Jake started yelling orders, because no-one else would.

Whatever, he surprised no-one more than himself when he suddenly shouted,

'You there, with the mules! Get goin'! We'll cover you!'

The short, muscular Mexican who'd been gripping the mules' lead rope bobbed his head quickly and jammed his heels into his horse's flanks. The animals took off right away and the mules trotted on with *federale* lead kicking up spurts of dust behind them.

The rest of the men had started shooting back at the soldiers at last. Jake did a quick head-count and came up with the figure seven, six Mexicans and Harry. He stabbed a finger at two of them, then singled out Harry, too. 'Go on with the mules! Quick now!'

'*Si jefe!*'

Harry held back. 'Jake — ?'

'Do it, kid! No matter what happens up here, get them guns back to Villa!'

The Englishman didn't want to go, that was plain. But Jake hissed, 'Do it, I said!' and that got him moving with the rest of them.

Jake's force was now down to four. Another of Villa's men back-flipped off his horse with a rose of blood blooming in the centre of his swarthy face. Three, then.

'Get off the trail!' he yelled in Spanish. '*Vamos!*'

The rocks and stunted trees weren't much, but they offered some cover, at least. Jake half-fell out of his saddle and quickly tethered his horse. Pablo's mount trotted past with Pablo still tied across its broad back. Jake stopped the animal just long enough to haul the dead man's Springfield .45/.70 from its sheath. He threw a look down the trail. He knew that he and the rest of them must stop these *federales* from getting their hands on the Lewis guns.

More lead chopped through the air and whined off the surrounding rocks, showering stone chips everywhere. He flinched, crouched, cursed and wondered what in hell's name he was doing down in this godforsaken wilderness anyway, fighting a war that was none of his damn' business in the first place.

But there was no time for any of that, not now. He thought briefly of Maggie, wondered if he would ever see her again

— and then he came around the rocks with the Springfield blazing. The *federales* were urging their horses down the narrow trail in a flatout charge now, firing handguns and yelling fit to bust. They must be desperate to stop those machine guns from reaching Villa to attempt such a foolish move.

Around Jake, the Mexicans started firing back at the charging *soldados*. For one endless moment there was nothing but the thunder and crack of weapons, the screams and cries of men and horses, boiling dust and trickling sweat and the hideous, metallic stench of fresh-spilled blood.

Then Jake surfaced from the melee like a swimmer coming up for air. The battle-rage left him and he saw everything as clear as a bell. Two of the *federales* out front of the charging column had stopped bullets and crashed backwards out of their saddles and right into the path of the pounding horses directly behind them. Two of the horses had stumbled and fallen over them, throwing their riders headlong. The trail ahead was

201

complete chaos. The soldiers were in disarray. But that didn't stop Jake and his men pouring more lead into them.

Another trooper fell out of his saddle, discharging his handgun by reflex into the sky. A horse reared up and fell, killed by a bullet in the eye. On the other side of the trail from Jake, one of the Mexicans yelped and went down, grabbing for his bullet-shattered right arm. One more *federale* slumped lifeless as a barrage of lead riddled his body and sent him twitching from this life into the next.

Jake had seen enough of it. Those *federales* up there were in such a wild tangle now that the last thing they were bothered about was a dozen Lewis guns.

He chanced a look around at his men. They were still triggering rounds at the soldiers with methodical, deadly precision. But this was no longer a battle: it was too one-sided for that.

'Mount up!' he bawled, deciding that enough was enough, that maybe they ought to get the hell out of here before reinforcements turned up. 'Mount up, I said! Come on! We're movin' out! *Now!*'

There was some sporadic fire from the surviving *federales,* but they were likely as shaken by the resistance they'd encountered as Jake was to have been a part of it. He helped the wounded man to mount up, then swung across leather and turned his own wall-eyed dun toward the northwest. Around him, the rest of Villa's men reluctantly followed his lead, one of them pausing to trigger a few parting shots into the confusion of the dead and dying, the wounded and the ragged survivors.

Jake kicked his horse to speed. His arms, back and legs throbbed dully, but the wind slipping past his sweat-run face felt good. Ahead, the narrow trail twisted this way and that, and his horse took every turn at reckless speed. When at last he hit a relatively straight run, he saw the string of mules and the four men with them just coming out onto the open plain below. They saw him, too. Harry hipped around and waved, and he reached up and waved back, urging them to keep going.

Despite the fact that his guts were

churning again, Jake allowed himself a moment of relief. For the first time it looked as if they were actually going to get away with it. Thundering hooves clattered on through the violent morning, bouncing back off the rocks surrounding him with a sound like . . . a sound like . . .

Huh?

Hunched over his horse's foamy neck, Jake screwed up his face, trying to identify the sound. Blood rushing through his ears? The drumming of the horses behind him? Sounds of pursuit? A bee, buzzing in his ear?

Down on the flatland below, Harry and the others were pointing at him and yelling. The Mexicans following him on his heady descent were starting to shout, too. What — ?

Suddenly the mysterious sound grew from a distant, angry whine into a sharp, ear-splitting roar. A black shadow fell across Jake and was gone in an instant. Startled, his horse broke stride and reared up, nickering and pawing the air. For a second or two, Jake thought the nag was going to toss him on his ass.

Then he saw what was making all the noise.

The Nieuport.

The *federales'* blasted biplane!

The infernal contraption roared over-head, double wings tipping first one way, then the other. It was flying about two hundred feet off the ground, following the angle of the rock- and brush-littered incline down towards the mules and riders below. Jake muttered an oath and fought the frightened dun to an uneasy standstill just as the remaining three Mexicans reined in behind him.

The Nieuport dove lower, its engine growling like a bobcat. It banked one way and Jake got a good look at its pale blue undercarriage. Then it banked the other, and he saw that the flimsy-looking thing was actually big enough to seat two men, the feller that drove it and another in back whose gloved hands were wrapped around a bolted-down Maxim machine gun.

A Maxim . . . Seized by a sudden dread, Jake whispered, 'Aw God, no.'

He watched, horror struck, as the

Nieuport flew ever lower, and Harry and the Mexicans below frantically began to search for cover. Only trouble was, there *wasn't* any cover down there, at least nothing that could conceal a man from someone up above.

The Nieuport sped closer. Its black shadow skittered across the uneven, brush-dotted ground beneath it. It skimmed right over the mules' heads, causing panic in men and animals alike, and then, as it was arcing up into the clear blue sky again, the machine-gunner in his brown leather cap and goggles let go with a burst from the Maxim gun.

'*No!*'

The machine gun's chatter drowned Jake's cry. The .75 calibre bullets tore up the ground around the men below. One of the Mexicans screamed as he and his horse were thrown sideways, both of them stitched by lead, to crash heavily against the hard-packed dirt.

One of the mules was hit, too. It toppled over, spilling its cargo with a splintery crack, its little grey legs kicking feebly as it died.

It was absolute chaos down there as Harry and the others fought to control their horses. The Nieuport went up, up, ever higher, its evil-sounding engine coughing and buzzing down across the hot plain until it finally came back around in a slow, almost leisurely arc, for a second run.

'*You bastard,*' Jake whispered in a shaky voice, unable to take his eyes off the diving biplane. 'Why, you cold-hearted *bastard!*'

The biplane swooped down on the defenseless men like some monstrous bird of prey. Harry grabbed his automatic and emptied his clip at it, but it did no good, no good at all . . .

The 'plane came in low and damn'-near took their heads off. As it snarled back up again, headed Jake's way, the machine-gunner let go another burst of .75s, and this time another mule fell, the feller leading them too, and Harry also tumbled from his rearing piebald to crash and roll in the dust.

Jake felt like puking. He had no stomach for slaughter, never had. But something quelled the sickly bubbling in his guts, something cold and grim that raced to the surface instead: a deadly, uncharacteristic craving for revenge.

Throwing caution to the wind, he kicked the dun into motion. The animal took off down the trail in a dusty blur. One of the Mexicans cried out, '*Señor! Señor!*' but Jake didn't even look back.

Behind him and someplace up above, the biplane was climbing again, readying itself for another dive. Out ahead, the trail stretched northwest in a lumpy, churned-up mess, split open by all that *federale* lead, and what had so recently been a group of men and animals now looked more like leftovers in an abattoir.

Jake's face was like murder as the dun left the foothills behind it and came thundering across the flats with dust exploding beneath its pounding hooves. Every broken-and-put-back-together bone in the wrangler's body was giving off waves of pain as the horse rose and fell beneath him, but still he kept going, racing towards the remnants of Harry's little band, bending forward over his horse's flying mane, feeling the sheer power of the animal between his legs as it propelled the pair of them ever closer.

At last he was there. He hauled on the reins and the dun skidded to a halt, tearing more chunks out of the already mutilated ground. Jake as good as fell out of the saddle. His legs almost gave way beneath him. He looked around quickly, saw one Mexican still struggling to control his horse, one mule still alive, two dead men —

'Harry?' Jake spun around. He could barely speak, he was breathing so hard. 'Harry?'

The young Englishman came up out of all the boiling dust on the other side of the trail, his round face smudged and his oiled brown hair askew. 'I'm . . . I'm all right, old chap,' he gasped. There was blood coursing down his forehead again, though, and when he hustled across to Jake, he was limping.

Jake switched his attention to the Nieuport. The biplane had reached the summit of its climb and was now coming around again in a wide sweep, to return for a third death-dealing pass.

'The bastard . . . ' Jake panted.

Harry put a hand on his arm. 'Jake . . . we . . . we've got to get away fr . . . from here.'

Jake cut a brief, cemetery glance at him and shook his head. 'An' go *where?*' he asked. 'Dammit, kid, there's nowhere!'

'Then what can we do?'

Jake's eyes fastened on one of the dead mules. The critter had spilled its load as it hit the ground, and one of the crates had split open.

'We can *fight*,' he hissed.

Harry followed him across to the edge of the trail and watched as Jake tore open part of the box-lid and hauled out one of the factory-new Lewis guns. Up above, still about half a mile away, the Nieuport finished its turn and started to swoop back down towards them, its engine howling banshee-like across the hills and flats.

Harry quickly inspected the gun in Jake's hands. At first glance it looked like a rifle, but its smooth barrel was too fat for that. The trigger mechanism looked odd, too: with a hand-grip not unlike the one on Harry's automatic.

'Oh, no!' he lamented. 'You're pulling my leg, Jake!'

Jake hefted the gun, testing the weight. ''Fraid not, kid.'

'But we don't even know how to use — '

'Look, jus' find me some ammo!'

They hauled the crate free of the dead mule and tore off the rest of the lid. While Jake hurriedly tried to fathom out the workings of the machine gun, Harry checked the box. 'Blast! Nothing else in here except for these circular things, Jake.'

Urgently Jake took a look for himself. 'That's it!'

'Eh?'

'That is the ammo, you idiot!'

The Nieuport was screaming down at them now, eating up the distance at an alarming rate. Jake fumbled one of the discus-sized magazines out of the box and tried to figure out where in hell it should go.

Harry solved the mystery. 'Try fitting it there, Jake.'

'Where?'

'There, on the top, just before you get to the barrel.'

Jake worked feverishly, with trembling hands, and almost dropped the magazine.

At last the thing clicked into place. He turned around to face the diving Nieuport with the stock of the light machine gun braced against his hip. His throat was tight and his palms were clammy. Very deliberately he brought the barrel up a little and tightened his trigger-finger . . .

Offering up a brief prayer, Jake let loose. The Lewis gun rattled out a message of death. The circular magazine on top spun furiously on its retaining pin. But nothing on earth could have prepared Jake for the recoil. Every time a cartridge was fired, it released enough gas to push back the bolt and feed down the next bullet. Consequently, the damn' gun jerked all over the place in his fists, sending shock-waves up his arms and across his shoulders that were too strong to ignore.

The pain of it was blinding. He yelled out and dropped the gun, staggering back a-ways, face screwed up as he cursed the crippled old-timer he had become.

The Nieuport was now near enough to reach out and touch. Harry pushed Jake aside and snatched up the gun, ignoring the heat of the barrel on his palm. His arms sagged at the weight of the weapon, but somehow he managed not to drop it.

'Swines!' he yelled at the oncoming 'plane. 'Sods! Buggers!'

Then he let them have it again. The Lewis gun belched flame. It coughed out bullets in a chattering stream. Jake drew his Peacemaker and emptied it at the 'plane. Beside him, the Englishman's entire frame shuddered with the machine gun's recoil.

Somehow he kept hold of the thing, though, kept the spitting barrel up and firing, and as the Nieuport screeched nearer he kept it blasting until the magazine was empty.

The biplane roared past, so low that its down-draught actually spilled them over. The machine-gunner let them have another burst of lead, but although it chopped up brush and dirt alike, it didn't even come close to where they were scrambling back to their feet.

'Give me another magazine!' Harry yelled.

Jake shuffled over to the crate. 'Here!'

Harry tore one of his fingernails trying to rip the spent magazine off the remaining pin and said, 'Oh . . . sugar!'

Together they fumbled the fresh magazine into place and turned to watch the biplane climbing quickly into the cloudless blue sky.

Except that it wasn't climbing.

Oh, it was *trying* to, sure: it just didn't seem able to manage it. The whine of the engine sounded different, too: higher, more uneven. It was coughing, shorting out, catching again, coughing some more. And that wasn't all.

Harry said, 'Look!'

Grey smoke was beginning to streak the sky behind the alternately dipping, then rising 'plane. When at last the thing turned — sluggishly, Jake thought — they saw that the smoke was coming from a point just behind the whirling propeller, that it wasn't just grey anymore, it was black, and that it was no longer just a streamer, but thick and getting thicker.

'Do you . . . ' Harry was almost afraid to ask the question, but he swallowed hard and tried again. 'Do you think that we've *done* it, Jake?'

Before Jake could reply, the Nieuport completed its turn and came roaring back at them, wings wagging, engine cutting out, then catching again.

'Only one way to make sure,' he growled.

Without a word, Harry braced the Lewis gun against his hip, brought the barrel up to line on the contraption coming toward them and set his mouth in a grim, determined line.

The surviving Mexican jumped down off his horse and raced over to join them, tossing Jake his 1895 Winchester and drawing his own Smith & Wesson Russian.

Behind them, the men Jake had left up in the foothills galloped in, dismounted, grabbed their long guns and ran over to add their own small firepower to that of the machine gun.

The 'plane hurtled towards them. Jake brought the Winchester up. 'Steady, now . . . steady . . . steady . . . *Fire!*'

The machine gun rattled. The circular magazine spun like a mad thing. Orange flame spewed from the smooth, fat barrel, and all of them lined up there with their guns up and blasting joined Harry in screaming their defiance at the *federale* 'plane bearing down on them, yelling for it to die, to die, to *die* . . .

The noise of it all was deafening. Gunfire, shouting, the high screech of the biplane's crippled engine: the mingling sounds were enough to burst a man's eardrums. But as loud as they were, they were dwarfed by the sound the 'plane made when it finally exploded.

It was about a hundred feet off the ground and three hundred feet away from them when it suddenly turned into a ball of bright white light. A sound like the end of the world shot out across the flatlands and knocked them all backwards again. Debris flew everywhere: nuts, bolts, batons of wood, strips of fiery canvas.

The double wings folded in on

themselves. One wheel shot off east across the desert. The entire flying machine disappeared in a red and orange conflagration and then tumbled earthward, exploding one final time as it impacted with the ground.

An enormous black wreath of smoke began to rise into the air, bruising the sky. Jake sagged a little. They all did. Harry dropped the Lewis gun and the two Mexicans flanking him both reached out to slap his back or shake his hand.

It should have been a moment of relief and celebration. They had won, after all. But Jake, ever the pragmatist, only saw all that thick, oily smoke as a beacon pinpointing their position to the enemy.

He listened to the spit and crackle of the hungry flames for a while, then said raggedly, 'Come on.' His throat was still hoarse from all that shouting. 'I reckon we've used up enough dumb luck for one day. Let's get the rest of these guns together an' get 'em back to Villa.'

And one of the Mexicans nodded respectfully and said, '*Si, jefe. En sequido!*'

★ ★ ★

'Gentlemen, I am in your debt,' Pancho Villa said just after dinner at Los Caballos Mestenos that evening. 'This business has been distasteful. It has cost us the lives of many good men. But without you, it would have cost us the Lewis guns as well.' He raised a fine crystal glass of Madeira in toast. 'If ever I can repay you . . .'

Jake picked up his own glass. Good food and fine wine had mellowed him a little after all the violence of the day, but the hard travelling it had taken to get back to relative safety had knocked most of the stuffing out of him, and all he wanted now was a soft bunk and eight hours' sleep.

'No disrespects, general,' he said, stifling a yawn. 'But we'd be just as happy to collect the balance of Elliott Blaze's money an' call it a day.'

Villa inclined his round head, and a knowing smile playing at the fleshy flips beneath his thick black moustache as he looked from Jake to Harry. 'I understand,' he replied. 'You have no stomach for the *revolucion*.'

'General,' Jake said without criticism, 'it's not our war. Harry here, he jus' wants to get to some place in California an' make movin' pictures. Me . . . ' His face grew troubled, and he let the sentence hang.

'Nevertheless,' Villa said in good humour, 'I salute you. For what it is worth, you have Villa's undying gratitude and respect, *señores*.'

The bandit general drank, and Jake and Harry joined him. Afterwards, with the balance of the money stowed safely in the tin box they'd taken from Miguel's saddlebags, the two Anglos crossed the dark, silent yard, heading towards the inky shadow that marked the position of the bunkhouse, both of them limping like a pair of old greybeards.

The night was cool and peaceful; the horror and death of that very same morning seemed a lifetime away.

'Not a bad fellow, old Villa,' Harry said expansively. 'For a foreigner, I mean.' He patted his stomach. 'Knows how to put on a decent spread, at any rate.' He glanced at his partner. 'Jake? Did you hear what I said?'

Jake cleared his throat. 'Uh? Oh . . . sure. You know somethin'?' he asked. 'You sound like you're kind of sorry this is all over.'

Harry showed surprise. 'Really? I can assure you that I'm not, old boy. Not in the least. No, if truth be told, I'm rather looking forward to returning to El Paso. I always did enjoy a good wedding.'

'Weddin'?'

Harry stopped walking and Jake did, too. The Englishman turned to face him and put a hand on his shoulder.

'Come on, Jake. I think I know you well enough by now to recognise when something's troubling you. You've been preoccupied ever since we got back here.' He paused, then said cautiously, 'It's your good lady, isn't it? Mrs Shaw?'

Jake made to deny it, then shrugged and did some non-committal muttering instead.

'Do you want the advice of a friend?' Harry asked gently.

Jake shrugged some more. 'I guess you'll give it whether I want it or not,' he said uncharitably.

'Yes,' Harry replied with a grin. 'I guess I will.'

'All right, then: let's hear it.'

'Well, it's short and sweet, really. If you love the woman, I think you ought to do something about it. I mean, thanks to this little affair, you've got money in the bank at last. It's not as if you couldn't *afford* to do the decent thing.'

Jake had already figured that out for himself. 'But what if she says no?' he asked helplessly. 'When I ask her?'

'She won't.'

'I wish I shared your confidence, kid.'

Harry chuckled. 'Believe me. Here, I'll tell you what I'll do. I'll even write a little speech for you.'

'Aw, I ain't no good at speechifyin'.'

'Don't worry. It won't be anything too flowery: just romantic enough to get the message across . . . '

'Forget it.'

Jake broke away from him and continued trudging toward the bunkhouse. Harry hustled after him. 'Oh, but you must, Jake!'

Jake pulled up sharp. 'Why?'

Harry said proudly, 'Because dialogue's always been my strongest point.'

They both stared at each other though the darkness. A long moment passed in silence. Then, very slowly, their faces began to shift and crease up as each of them started laughing hard enough to split his sides.

★ ★ ★

Early in 1914, when much of the rest of the world was just about to become involved in the so-called Great War, and Harry Stanford-Brown abandoned his dreams of writing moving pictures in order to return home and fight for his country, the uneasy alliance between Pancho Villa, Emiliano Zapata and Venustiano Carranza began its concerted push against the corrupt and dictatorial General Victoriano Huerta.

In 1915 — the same year that the United States finally lifted its arms embargo — the ousted Huerta was forced to flee Mexico City and take up residence abroad.

Three days after leaving Los Caballos Mestenos, Jake Tanner rode into El Paso, and after finding Maggie working down at E.B. Taylor's eatery, dragged her out into the backyard, fished out a sheet of paper filled with Harry's hasty scribble and embarked upon his proposal of marriage.

He got halfway through comparing Mags to a summer's day before he lost his nerve. Screwing the sheet of paper up into a ball, he said, 'Aw, hell, Mags. You know what I'm tryin' to say.'

She said, 'Yes.'

He regarded her from beneath lowered eyebrows. 'So?' he prompted, dry-mouthed. 'What . . . ah . . . what's your answer? 'Bout the two of us gettin' spliced?'

Maggie looked up into his long, trail-worn face. The heat from E.B.'s stove had flushed her cheeks a delicate pink, and one lock of her dyed blonde hair hung limp across her forehead. She looked very serious as she regarded him. Then she smiled.

'Are you going deaf or something, Jake?' she asked, reaching out to take both of his hands in hers. 'I just told you, didn't I?'

Relief coursed through him. He could hardly believe his luck. Impulsively he pulled her to him, thinking that she had never felt nor smelled so good, and he pressed her to his chest in a fierce, heartfelt embrace.

After a week in hell, he'd finally come home to paradise — and damned if that wasn't exactly where he intended it to stay.

THE END